A PLACE TO CALL HOME

**TOBY'S
TALE**

G.A. WHITMORE

outskirtspress
DENVER, COLORADO

This book is dedicated to Toby and to all rescue dogs in need of a place to call home.

Toby
1988 - 1999

A portion of the proceeds from the sale of each book will be donated to either the Humane Society of the United States or an organization of the author's choice that has demonstrated successful efforts in promoting and advocating for the protection and welfare of dogs.

ACKNOWLEDGEMENTS

My sincere thanks to Mary Gladue for gently guiding me in the right direction. Thanks to Beth Bruno for making sure all my i's were dotted and my t's were crossed. Glen, you know who you are, as I said before, you rescued me. Colleen, you were my saving grace, and I want to thank you for all your support and encouragement. I don't think I would have gotten to this point without you. Dad and Terry, thank you for being such good friends to Toby. I know the three of you are together again. And lastly, Cory, thanks for believing in your Mutti and always keeping the faith that I could do this.

Please consider adopting from your local shelter if you have room in your heart and home for a rescue dog. Visit my website at *http://www.gawhitmore.com/* for a list of shelters in your area.

PROLOGUE

Toby huddled beneath the small table in the corner of the room. His eyes darted back and forth in fear. The corner, at one time a place of refuge, a place to escape from the man and his wrath, had now become a trap. Except for the uncontrollable trembling coursing through his body, he remained perfectly still. Pain emanated from the point where the man's boot had made contact with his leg, his right leg this time.

As the yelling around him continued, his resolve to run away strengthened. Although he had found love and friendship at this place he had begun to think of as home, he had found pain and suffering as well. He closed his eyes, shut out the noise, and transported himself back to the safe shelter of the farm. Back to his mother and his sister Tara. Back to a time of no pain . . .

PART I
THE FAMILY TREE

✧   ✧   ✧

"When a shepherd goes to kill a wolf,
and takes his dog along to see the sport,
he should take care to avoid mistakes.
The dog has certain relationships to the wolf
the shepherd may have forgotten."

– Robert Persig

CHAPTER 1

TOBY AND SHEP DASHED into the cool, dark barn. Bits of straw fell from their fur as they sprinted across the dirt floor, racing to where their mother lay feeding the others. In their wake, clouds of dust particles danced and swirled in the beams of sunlight streaming through the open hayloft doors above. Playing with his brother had made Toby hungry, but Shep reached their mother first and beat him to the last feeding spot. He pushed his way through the squirming bodies of his siblings, hoping to dislodge one of them . . .

"Hey!" someone yelled. "You're stepping on me!"

"Sorry, Tuck, but I'm starving." Out of all of them, why did he have to pick Tuck to step on?

"You're not the only one who's hungry," his brother snapped. "First come, first served. Now get off me and wait your turn." Toby lost his footing as Tuck settled back down to feed and, as luck would have it, found himself at an empty feeding spot between two of his other siblings.

The morning was an unusually hot one, even for July. The strong summer sun beat down on Missy and her puppies. The heat didn't seem to bother the puppies the way it bothered Missy, who, at the moment of Toby's triumph, decided to move out of the path of the hot rays. The puppies had been feeding long enough. She pulled herself up from the mass of fur balls at her stomach, forcing Toby to let go of her. Feeding time was over.

The litter was Missy's second. The puppies from her first litter had been sold shortly after they were born. She still missed them terribly, and always would, but the new puppies kept her busy, especially Toby and Tara. She had a special place in her heart for them. The only two white puppies amongst a brood of all black, they stood out from the rest of the pack like missing front teeth. And even though Toby was the largest of the litter, he didn't act the part. His temperament was mild, and he never used his size to bully his siblings. Missy suspected he wasn't even aware of his intimidating appearance. Tara—smaller than Toby, but still larger than their other siblings—stuck to Toby like his shadow wherever he went. The two were inseparable.

✧ ✧ ✧

THE LARGE BAILEY farm where Missy and her family lived was like most farms. A large white house sat proudly at the front of the property, which abutted the dirt road leading to the main street into town. Behind the house was a faded, red barn surrounded by numerous outbuildings. Cows and sheep grazed in the fields, and the sound of chickens clucking and garbling emanated from the coops behind the barn. In the distance, two horses fed in the meadow that stretched out to the woods that encircled the property.

Generations of Baileys had made their living farming and raising livestock, first in the small town of Cookes Crossing, Idaho, and then in northern California, where the current Bailey family had moved just two years earlier. The Baileys—or rather, Mr. Bailey, to be precise—had decided to move the family with the hope of improving their financial situation. Mrs. Bailey was still waiting for them to reap the benefits of that decision.

Mr. Bailey had started breeding German Shepherds several years earlier, and though it was a side business for him, he took it very seriously. His reputation for selling high quality dogs grew with each litter, and he even received inquiries from out-of-state buyers who were willing to travel long distances to purchase a "Bailey Breeders" dog. But when the last litter produced two more white puppies, Mr. Bailey was livid. He still believed—as many breeders still did—that white German Shepherds were an anomaly, a genetic defect of the breed.

That morning, as Toby struggled to find a spot to eat, the Bailey family sat together eating breakfast, quietly enjoying the standard fare of bacon and eggs Mrs. Bailey had prepared.

Mr. Bailey popped the last piece of toast into his mouth, pushed his chair back from the table and stretched his legs.

"There goes our profit from this litter," he said, breaking the silence that had settled at the table. "All of the puppies would've been sold by now if it weren't for those two white ones. We've always been able to find buyers for all of the puppies well before they were ready to go, at least up until that last white puppy born two years ago. In fact, we usually have to turn people away." He shook his head in disgust. "We'll never find anyone to buy those two." The scowl on his leathery face matched the deep wrinkles etched there. His pale green eyes, barely visible between the squinted slits of his lids, peered out beneath bushy auburn eyebrows.

"Someone will buy them," said Mrs. Bailey, pausing her fork in midair. "They're adorable."

"How can you say that? It took us forever to find someone to buy the last one and look what happened there," he shot back at her, absentmindedly brushing the toast crumbs that had fallen onto the bib of his faded overalls onto the equally faded linoleum floor. "Besides, I'm more worried about my reputation being tarnished than getting rid of those dogs."

Michael had stopped eating as soon as his father mentioned the two white puppies. Why was his father always so angry about them? They were the cutest puppies he had ever seen. How could they make anyone angry?

"Why won't anyone want them?" Michael asked. "They're so cute, and they're really smart, too." Innocence shone on his small freckled face. He was smaller than most boys his age. And if that wasn't enough, he had inherited his father's red hair, which made him stand out like a beacon wherever he went. Some of the older kids at school liked to tease him and called him "carrot-top" or "freckle-face". He tried not to let the razzing bother him; sometimes he would even laugh with them to hide the hurt he felt inside.

Mr. Bailey turned to his son. "Trust me. No one wants a white German Shepherd."

"Then can *we* keep them, Dad? Please?" Michael's soft hazel eyes pleaded with his father.

"Absolutely not," said Mr. Bailey. "It's out of the question. Now finish your breakfast so you can do your chores."

Michael knew from experience that the discussion was over. He would pretend the puppies were his for the time being, which, if nobody wanted to buy them, might be a long time.

Later that afternoon, as Michael half-heartedly swept the front porch, he tried to think of names for the two white dogs but none of the ideas he came up with satisfied him. On his way to clean out the horse stable, he stopped to sit on the wooden swing that hung from the old tree in the back yard. As he slowly swung back and forth, the toes of his old sneakers scraping the dirt beneath him, his mind drifted to thoughts of his friends and how much he missed them now that school was over. Since his friends' farms were so far away from his own, recess was one of the few opportunities he had to play with them during the school year, and in the summer, he rarely saw them at all. Playing with the puppies helped alleviate the loneliness he sometimes felt.

One of the games he and his friends liked to play during recess was cowboys and Indians. They would use sticks for guns and arrows and run around the school-yard whooping and hollering. Most of his friends preferred being cowboys, but Michael always chose to be an Indian.

"I know," he said suddenly, "I'll give them Indian names. I'll name the boy puppy Little Chief and the girl puppy White Cloud." Michael smiled to himself and ran off to tell his friend Walt, the farmhand.

CHAPTER 2

MISSY HAD BEEN waiting for the right time to tell Toby and Tara about their heritage. The two white puppies were the embodiment of the legacy that had been passed down to them. As a young puppy, Missy had never tired of hearing the story of how her mother and father had met and, in spite of the challenges and obstacles they had faced, had fallen in love and had a family. She would listen raptly each time her mother recounted the tale. Missy knew that the time had come for her to pass the story of their grandparents down to Toby and Tara.

So later that day, as Mr. Bailey grumbled about the white puppies to Walt, the two objects of his ire listened to their mother, spellbound, as she began the tale . . .

Sadie was two months old when she arrived at the Bailey farm in Cookes Crossing, Idaho. The new surroundings frightened her and the loneliness she felt from missing her family consumed her waking moments. But eventually she began to make friends with the other farm animals, and her loneliness lessened a little each day as she settled into her new life.

Soon after her first litter was sold, Sadie began to wander from the farm into the woods surrounding the crop fields. A heavy sorrow had laid itself upon her after her puppies were taken away one by one, and her trips into the woods—away from the noise and bustle of the farm—helped lessen her grief. Sometimes she would be gone for hours.

One day, a day that up to this point had passed like most others, Sadie rose from the warm patch of sun on the front porch of the farmhouse. She slowly stretched her front and back legs, shook out her fur, then sniffed the air in the direction of the woods. A moment later, when the farmer's wife came out onto the porch, Sadie was gone.

She started down the usual trail north of the farm and stopped now and then to drink in the rich, earthy smells of autumn that enveloped her. A slight chill in the air reminded her that winter was on its way. Sadie picked up her pace and arrived at the path that led to a small stream. Its cool, clear water tasted better than the water the woman left in her pen each day.

When she reached the last curve in the path before the stream's clearing, she immediately detected an unfamiliar scent; the scent of another animal. The soft, damp soil beneath her paws muffled her steps as she moved closer to its source.

She stopped. A large animal stood at the edge of the stream drinking from the flowing water. Sadie was close enough to hear the thirsty lapping of the creature's tongue.

She had come across other animals in the woods before, but never one like this. Never one so large. Her body tensed. The sights, smells, and sounds around her intensified as adrenalin coursed through her veins. Part of her wanted to turn and run, but the magnificence of the creature held her captive and drew her forward.

His thick, white fur was touched with streaks of gold, and the splintered sunlight that broke through the leafy boughs of the trees lining the far side of the stream danced upon him so he appeared to sparkle like rippling water reflecting the sun. His most striking feature was his long, thick tail that swept up in a curve at the end as if to avoid touching the ground. Mesmerized, Sadie didn't notice the small twig on the path as she involuntarily stepped closer.

Strider detected Sadie's scent a split second before he heard the twig snap. He whipped his head around, ears erect, senses alert and found himself facing an animal whose likeness he had never seen before. She was not a wolf, though she had wolf-like features and wolf-like fur. Fur that was as black as the many moonless nights he had recently traveled.

As he moved closer to her, he detected another scent—an all too familiar one—the scent of humans. Understanding dawned on him like the first ray of the sun breaking through the morning sky. Strider knew of her kind—dogs they were called. Dogs lived with humans. His mother had been killed by a human when he was just a pup and several of this creature's kind had been part of the hunt. His father, the pack's leader, had warned him to stay away from dogs. "Where there are dogs, there are humans. And though *dogs are descended from our kind, they have forgotten the true ways of wolves, the ways of hunting and surviving in the wilderness. They are weak and bring shame to our kind by depending on humans for their existence."*

Strider was certain he now faced one of these creatures. A low, menacing growl rose from his throat.

Sadie froze when the animal turned toward her. "I'm . . . I'm sorry for disturbing you," she said, breaking the heavy tension that filled the air. Her voice betrayed her fear. She took a step back. "When I saw you I . . ." her voice trailed off. Strider stopped growling and looked at her, his head cocked.

"Who are you? Where did you come from?" he demanded.

"My . . . my name is Sadie. I'm from the farm . . ." she said, and took another step back.

"What farm? How far is it from here?"

His deep, gruff voice frightened her. "It's up the trail . . . that way." She turned her head in the direction of the farm and quickly turned back. "I was taking a walk . . ." Sadie hesitated. While talking, she had managed to move several feet back up the path.

"I stop by here to get a drink sometimes," she continued. "I'll just go now and leave you alone." Sadie was barely able to keep herself from bolting away.

"Wait," Strider commanded. "I can smell humans on you. Do you live with humans?"

"Yes," Sadie responded cautiously. "They own the farm I live on. I was taken away from my family when I was young and brought there to live."

"Why don't you escape? You've come this far with no

humans nearby; why don't you just keep going?" Strider's eyes narrowed. "Do you like living with them?"

Her fear of him deepened. She opened her mouth to speak, but no sound came out.

"Don't you know what humans do to other animals?" he asked without waiting for an answer. "They kill and maim them for no reason. I know. They killed my mother." Strider's head dropped, and his body sagged slightly from the burden of the painful memory. When he finally raised his gaze to her, the look on Sadie's face had transformed from one of fear to one of sympathy.

"I'm sorry," she said.

The genuine compassion in her voice caught Strider by surprise. His guard crumbled. Maybe his father was wrong. Maybe all dogs were not alike.

"I'm sorry, too," he said. "I'm sorry for judging you so harshly." He cocked his head and studied her. "I've never met a dog before. I didn't know what to expect. I hope you'll forgive me. My name is Strider." He bowed slightly toward Sadie.

"I haven't seen you here before. Where are you from?" she asked timidly.

"I was born in a land far north of here. I like to travel and see new places. What about you? What brings you to these woods?" He found he wanted to learn more about her.

"I started venturing away from the farm last spring after my puppies were . . . were taken from me." Sadie's voice dropped at the end.

"Who took your puppies from you?" Strider asked in alarm.

"The farmer. He sold them."

"He sold them?" he asked in disbelief.

"Yes, it's one of the ways he makes money, by breeding dogs and then selling them. That's why he bought me, to have puppies for him to sell."

"Oh," replied Strider, contemplating what she had told him.

"It's not so bad, I guess," she continued. "The farmer and his wife treat me good, and the puppies always seem to like the people who buy them." She hesitated. "I miss them though." They both stood silent for a moment.

"I need to get back to the farm now," Sadie said. "If I'm gone too long, they'll start to look for me."

"Will you meet me here again tomorrow so we can talk some more?" Strider asked. "If you'd like to, that is."

"I'd like to."

"I'll see you tomorrow then?"

"Tomorrow," Sadie replied, and turned back up the trail. Her impulse was to run, but she refrained from doing so until she was out of Strider's view, then she bolted like a bullet back to the farm. Strider watched her disappear into the trees. His ideas about dogs changed forever.

Each afternoon, from that day forward, Sadie and Strider met at the clearing by the stream. They spent their time sharing stories or just relaxing in each other's company. Strider recounted tales of his travels and adventures while Sadie listened with wide-eyed wonderment. Her desire to experience her own adventures grew stronger with each tale he told.

As the days and weeks passed, a strong friendship

developed between the two. Winter came and they continued to meet in a small cave Strider had discovered a short distance from the stream. By midwinter, their relationship had blossomed from one of friendship, into one of love.

CHAPTER 3

WINTER PASSED AND slowly melted into spring. As the days grew warmer, Sadie realized she was going to have another litter. She couldn't wait to tell Strider the news. He had asked Sadie if she would travel back north with him to live with his pack, and without hesitation she had said yes. Strider warned her that the trip would be difficult and at times potentially dangerous, but Sadie didn't care about the danger; she just wanted to be with him. They planned to depart as soon as spring had a firm grip on the land, and though she already felt more tired than usual, her pregnancy didn't alter her desire to leave; if anything, it strengthened it. She knew the puppies would be sold if she stayed at the farm. Sadie would not let that happen again.

The morning had been an especially tiring one for Sadie, and she decided to rest until it was time for her to meet Strider. She lay down in the barn and let her thoughts turn to their upcoming journey as she drifted off to sleep . . .

The pleasant scents of the woods permeated the air. Sadie took a deep breath. Though the woods were unfamiliar, she was comforted by Strider's presence beside her as they walked down the well-worn path. When they came to where the path narrowed, Strider stepped aside and let Sadie go ahead. The path veered to the left around an outcrop of rock. As she passed the imposing stone formation, the peace was suddenly broken by the sound of humans shouting nearby. She turned to Strider; he was gone.

Fear gripped her.

The scene in the woods evaporated as Sadie opened her eyes and found herself lying on her bed of hay inside the barn. The woods—the smells, the sounds—they had all been part of a dream, but the sound of humans yelling continued. Panic seized her. She sprang up and ran out of the barn. Before she had gone more than a few feet, a gunshot rang out, piercing the quiet afternoon. The shot was instantly followed by a horrible, wailing howl. Strider's howl.

Before Sadie could react, she heard the click of the leash hook onto her collar and looked up to see the farmer's wife bending over her. The sound of Strider's howl continued to echo in Sadie's ears.

Strider had waited for Sadie at the clearing by the stream for close to an hour before he decided to go look for her. He could not shake the fear that something terrible had happened. She had never been late before. Strider approached the farm warily.

At the edge of the woods, he stopped to study the layout

of the farm. Beyond the crop fields he could see the barn where Sadie had told him she slept, but there was no sign of her. Strider sniffed the air several times, but the wind was not in his favor, and only the familiar scents of the forest reached him.

The situation appeared hopeless. There was no way to approach the barn without the risk of being seen. The fields held no cover, for they had only recently been planted. He considered returning later that evening after darkness had fallen and the humans slept.

Strider began to pace as he agonized over what to do. He heard a human yell and quickly turned toward the sound. A man stood by the barn pointing at him. A second man ran around the corner of the building with a shotgun in his hand. Strider knew what a shotgun looked like and what it was used for; his father had taught him well. As he turned to flee back into the woods, the crack of a gunshot split the air.

A sharp, searing pain consumed him. He involuntarily let out a howl that filled the echoing silence. A second shot exploded. Strider heard the bullet whizz by.

Time was his enemy now. The humans would hunt him down. He limped into the cover of the brush and glimpsed at his wound. Bright red blood stained the white fur where the bullet had hit his leg. The pain was excruciating, but he knew he had to keep going if he wanted to live.

When he reached the clearing by the stream, he stopped to look at the wound more closely. Even though the bullet had not lodged in his leg, enough of his skin and muscle had been grazed to leave an ugly, gaping sore. Instinctively, Strider stepped into the stream and moved to where the water was deep enough to cover the gash. At first the water stung the raw flesh, but the coolness felt good against the hot, burning pain.

As he stood there, Strider frantically pondered his next move. He couldn't go back to the farm now, not even under the cover of darkness, for his wound would prevent a quick escape if he were spotted. The only thing to do was leave the area until his wound healed and then come back for Sadie. With his decision made, he waded out of the stream and shook himself off.

"I'll be back for you, Sadie," Strider vowed, as he looked down the path to the farm and reluctantly headed in the opposite direction.

✧　✧　✧

MR. BAILEY STRUGGLED to untangle the large roll of chicken wire stored behind the barn. He stood up to stretch his back and spotted Strider at the edge of the woods.

"Get the gun, Charlie!" he yelled. "There's a wolf out by the cornfield. Hurry up!"

Hearing her husband yell out to the farmhand, Mrs. Bailey dropped the clothespin she had just picked up and ran over to the barn. Charlie came running out with a hunting rifle in the crook of his arm.

Mr. Bailey turned to his wife.

"Go tie up the dog. There's a wolf at the edge of the corn field. Hurry up!" She ran into the barn to get Sadie.

Years of hunting came to Charlie's aid, and he quickly raised the gun, caught the wolf in its sight, and pulled the trigger. A blast rang out across the field. Charlie could tell by the wolf's sudden jerking motion that the bullet had struck its mark, and the howl that immediately followed proved him correct.

"You got him, Charlie!" Mr. Bailey yelled. "Take another shot! He's running back into the woods!" A second shot rang out. No howl followed this time; the wolf had disappeared. Charlie lowered the gun to his side.

"You missed him that time, but not by much," said Mr. Bailey. "If he doesn't bleed to death, he'll die from the next bullet if he ever shows up around here again. We'd better tighten up security for the farm animals until we're sure he's not coming back. An injured wolf can be awful mean."

Mrs. Bailey spoke soothingly to Sadie as she walked her over to the fenced-in area beside the barn. "Mr. Bailey thinks you should stay in the pen for a while so you'll be safe from that poor wolf Charlie shot. He's probably right, even though I know you won't be happy stuck in here."

Once inside the pen, Mrs. Bailey bent down to unhook the leash. Her long, dark hair, which she usually wore tied back, fell into her face. She stood up to gather the errant strands to the side and accidently dropped the end of the leash. Before she realized what had happened, Sadie dashed through the still-open gate.

"Lucy! Come back!" Mrs. Bailey yelled at Sadie. (Lucy was the name Mrs. Bailey had given Sadie when they first bought her, a name Sadie didn't like at all.)

"What's going on?" Mr. Bailey asked, as he came out of the barn.

"Lucy ran off toward the woods right where the wolf was shot."

"Fool dog," scowled Mr. Bailey. "She's going to go and get herself killed. I suppose we have to go find her."

By now, Sadie had vanished into the trees, the long leash trailing behind her.

✧ ✧ ✧

SADIE ENTERED THE woods and immediately headed toward the stream. The leash, still hooked onto her collar, dragged behind her as she ran. When she finally reached the clearing, she could smell Strider's scent, but there was no sign of him. She frantically scanned the surrounding area. He must have gone to the cave, she thought, but she was too exhausted to make the trip there. The pregnancy sapped her energy, and she needed a few minutes to rest before pushing on.

✧ ✧ ✧

CHARLIE SPOTTED Sadie lying next to the stream. She appeared to be sleeping. He moved quietly up the trail until he was only a few feet away from the end of her leash. He shot forward and grabbed it before she could react.

CHAPTER 4

THE FIRST DAY OF summer heralded the birth of three healthy puppies, one female and two males. The female and one of the males were black like Sadie, but the other male was the spitting image of Strider. Sadie, once again confined with the puppies in the pen next to the barn, was miserable. Her imprisonment prevented her from searching for Strider. The only reprieve from her anguish came from taking care of the puppies. At least once a day she would tell them the story of how she had met their father. The puppies would listen intently until their little eyelids began to droop and they fell off to sleep.

Sadie pushed her nose through one of the openings in the chain-link fence. The result was always the same: nothing. Trying to dig her way out of the enclosure had also proven fruitless. The ground was too hard. She lay down on the smoothly packed dirt in the corner of the pen. The three puppies ran to her, each claiming a feeding spot. Sadie closed her eyes and sighed. Her thoughts turned to Strider as the puppies squirmed and pushed at her tender belly. He would be so proud of them, she thought. Where is he? Is he alive? Will I ever see him again?

✧　✧　✧

MR. BAILEY WAS NOT surprised by Sadie's pregnancy. He had bred her shortly after the incident with the wolf. The stud—for whose services he had paid dearly—came from one of the best line of German Shepherds around, so he was shocked when one of them was born pure white. It was a very upsetting development for Mr. Bailey, who saw one third of his profits from the litter evaporate.

"If I had wanted to breed white German Shepherds, I would've bred her with that stupid wolf that was hanging around here a while back," he grumbled to Mrs. Bailey several weeks after the puppies were born. He and his wife were sitting in the living room, as they did each evening after Michael went to bed.

"Nevertheless," Mrs. Bailey commented absentmindedly, "he's a handsome dog."

"Handsome or not, it doesn't matter," her husband responded. "We have to get rid of him. If we can't sell him, I don't know what we're going to do."

"By the way," Mrs. Bailey asked. "When are you going to let Lucy out of that pen? She's been miserable since she's been in there. I'm worried about her."

"Well, I suppose that wolf would've come back by now if he was gonna come back at all. I don't know what a white wolf was doing around here anyway. I'll let her out during the day, but at night I think she should stay in the pen," Mr. Bailey said. "By the way, I have to go into town tomorrow to pick up some supplies I ordered. While I'm there, I'll stop at the post office and put an ad on the board to see if anyone wants to buy that white puppy. Maybe someone will respond. They're coming to pick up the black male this weekend. It's too bad those others changed their mind about buying this one." He nodded toward the young female asleep in Mrs. Bailey's lap. "But I've been thinking maybe we should keep her as another breeding dog. She's real pretty. Looks a lot like Lucy, huh?"

"She sure does," replied Mrs. Bailey. "She's the spitting image of her." There was no reason for her husband to know that she had already decided to keep her.

Two weeks later, after the Baileys had finished eating breakfast, the call came.

Mr. Bailey answered the phone. "Hello?"

"Hi, my name's Ned Johnson. I'm calling about the ad you have at the post office for the white German Shepherd puppy."

"Are you interested in seeing him?" Mr. Bailey inquired, trying to hide his excitement at the prospect of a possible buyer for the dog. No sense in giving away the farm.

"Yes, I am, but I'm just visiting the area until the weekend. I was wondering if you'd have time for me to come out to see him this afternoon?"

"Sure, no problem," Mr. Bailey replied. "I'll be here all day."

"How about around two?" Mr. Johnson asked.

"Two it is," said Mr. Bailey, and he proceeded to give Mr. Johnson directions to the farm. He hung up the phone and turned to his wife. "Maybe our luck has changed. The guy that just called might be interested in buying the white puppy."

Without looking up from the newspaper she was reading, Mrs. Bailey said, "That's great news, honey." If she had known the dramatic consequences the arrival of Mr. Johnson would have for Sadie and her puppy, she would have reacted differently.

✦   ✦   ✦

SADIE, NOW FREE from the confinement of her pen during the day, took time each afternoon to search for signs of Strider while the puppies were sleeping, and the day that Mr. Johnson visited the farm was no exception. Almost four months had passed since Strider had been shot, and Sadie refused to let go of her belief that he was still alive.

The day, comfortably warm and full of promise, brimmed with the scents of the season: the newly cut crops in the fields, the abundant vegetation of the woods, and the rich loam of the well-worn path she traveled.

When she arrived at the clearing before the stream, she immediately recognized Strider's scent. Joy erupted within her. "Strider's alive!" she cried out. "He's alive! I can smell him. He's been here recently. Today!" Sadie could barely contain herself. Tracks were visible in the wet ground by the water. But where was he?

A sound on the path behind her caused Sadie to turn, but the sun momentarily blinded her. Floating like a specter through the brilliant light, a vague form moved toward her. A familiar voice cried out from the mirage.

"Sadie, you're here! I've been waiting for you!"

"Strider, it's you! It's really you!" Sadie cried out in joy. "I thought I was seeing things, that the sun was playing tricks on me. But it's really you! You're alive!" Tears flowed from her eyes and washed away the weeks and months of pain and anguish that had weighed on her soul.

"I've missed you so much!" she said, lovingly looking him over.

Strider had changed. He seemed older, more mature. Something of substance had altered within him. His eyes, especially, reflected the transformation. Sadie knew she had similarly changed, for they had traveled the path of adversity together.

"Where have you been all this time? I've been so worried about you. I wouldn't accept the fact that you might be . . . dead."

"I had to leave, Sadie. The pain from the bullet wound . . . it was too much. I had to let the wound heal before I came back to get you. Let's leave this place, Sadie, today, right now. There's no reason to wait; we've had to wait long enough." Strider's voice was filled with urgency.

"Strider," Sadie said. "There's something I need to tell you first."

"What is it? What's wrong? You still want to go with me, don't you?" he asked, afraid of the answer.

"Of course I do, now more than ever. I never want to be away from you again."

Relief coursed through Strider.

"What is it then?"

She hesitated and then said, "We're parents. I was going to tell you the day you were shot, but . . ." She stopped, not sure how he would react to the news. "I gave birth to three puppies while you were gone. You're a father."

"I'm a father?" he echoed her in disbelief. "Oh, Sadie, that's wonderful! I can't believe it! I want to see them. Where are they?"

"Slow down. I can't keep up with you." Sadie laughed for the first time in a long while. It felt good. "There are three of them: Seth, who looks just like you, and Missy and Jordan. They both have black fur like me." She then hesitated and tears welled up in her eyes again. "But Jordan . . ." she started; her voice broke.

"Did something happen to Jordan?" Strider asked.

"Jordan was taken away. They came and took him the other day," Sadie said, holding back the tears that threatened to spill out.

"Who took him?"

"The family that came to see the puppies a few weeks ago. The two children loved Jordan, and he seemed to like them, too."

"Oh, Sadie, I'm sorry you had to go through that. It must have been so difficult for you." He waited a moment and then asked, "What about Seth and Missy? Do you think the farmer plans to sell them, too?"

"I don't know. I think they want to keep Missy. The woman is always taking her into the house with her. But I'm worried about Seth. The older he gets, the more he looks like you. What if the farmer figures out the puppies are yours? Oh, Strider, what are we going to do?"

"That settles the issue," Strider said firmly. "We have to leave here, Sadie. Immediately. It's more important than ever now, and we have to take Missy and Seth with us. They'll slow us down, but it doesn't matter as long as we're together. We have to get them away from the farm."

"I'll sneak away with them tonight while the family is eating their supper," Sadie suggested. "You can wait for us here by the stream. But you must promise not to come to the farm. Not after what happened the last time. I can't lose you again."

"I promise. I'll wait for you here in the woods."

"No matter how long it takes us to get here?"

"No matter how long it takes."

Sadie thought about how lucky she was as she ran back to the farm. Strider was alive, and their life together could finally begin. She would see new lands, meet Strider's family, and become a part of that family. Anxious for nightfall to come and the adventure to begin, Sadie ran faster.

CHAPTER 5

MR. JOHNSON SHOWED up at the Bailey farm at exactly two o'clock that afternoon. Mr. Bailey, who had been sitting on the front porch, rose to greet him.

"I appreciate you letting me come here on such short notice," Mr. Johnson said, and held out his hand. Mr. Bailey reached out and shook it. "I've been interested in purchasing a white German Shepherd ever since my brother bought one. They're real smart dogs, pretty too, hard to find, though."

"Well, let me show him to you. Follow me." Mr. Bailey led the way to the barn, still puzzled as to why anyone would want to buy a white German Shepherd. "I'd like to see the mother, too. Is she around?" Mr. Johnson asked.

"She's somewhere. Now that the puppies are bigger, she's started taking off into the woods again every day around this time. I don't know what the attraction is. She used to be gone for hours last spring until that wolf came around," Mr. Bailey commented.

"You have a lot of wolves around here?" Mr. Johnson inquired.

"I've seen a couple. I never saw one that was all white like this one, though."

The puppies were asleep when Mr. Bailey and Mr. Johnson reached the pen, but the sound of the men's voices awakened them.

"Here they are. They're healthy dogs. Big for their age," Mr. Bailey said.

"The white one sure is big," Mr. Johnson said, as he picked up the puppy and examined him closely. "How old did you say he is?"

"Eleven weeks," Mr. Bailey replied.

Mr. Johnson continued to examine the puppy.

"Are his parents white, too?"

"No, they're both black and tans," replied Mr. Bailey.

"Are you sure the parents are both purebreds?"

"Of course I'm sure they're both purebreds," Mr. Bailey replied defensively. "I saw the father's papers and I've used him before. I paid enough for him. He's the best German Shepherd stud around these areas. And the mother's as pure as they come. Why do you ask?" Mr. Bailey questioned, uncertain what Mr. Johnson was implying. "You said on the phone you wanted a white German Shepherd."

"Yes, I did, and I do. He sure is a beauty. Very striking features. How much do you want for him?"

"Two hundred."

"I'll give you $150," Mr. Johnson countered.

"He's yours." Mr. Bailey reached out and shook the man's hand.

WHEN SADIE EMERGED from the woods on the edge of the crop field, she immediately noticed the unfamiliar truck parked next to the barn where she had left the puppies sleeping in the corner of the pen.

She stopped.

Fear gripped her. Her heart began to pound. Did someone come to take one of their puppies? She hesitated only a moment before sprinting toward the barn, but the distance was too great.

She watched helplessly as the stranger picked Seth up and placed him in a small box. He carried the box over to the truck and put it in the back cargo area. The stranger exchanged a few words with the farmer and got into the vehicle.

"Oh no!" she cried. "He's taking Seth!" She heard the engine start and watched helplessly as the truck drove past the house and turned down the dirt road to town.

Sadie's maternal instincts compelled her to run after the truck, to go help Seth, but she knew she couldn't help him by herself. She needed Strider. She turned and bolted back down the path desperately yelling for Strider. As she approached the turn to the stream, she heard Strider's responding call and saw him dashing down the trail to meet her.

"Strider, there's a man," Sadie blurted out between labored breaths. "He took Seth . . . He put him in a box . . . in the back of his truck. We need to hurry!"

They sprang away in the direction of the dirt road that now carried Seth away from them. Strider barely touched the ground as his lean, muscular body flew down the path. He ran faster than he ever had before; trees and brush rushed past him. Errant branches that crossed his path easily gave way to his body as he crashed through the inconsequential obstacles. The distance between Sadie and him grew quickly. He turned to glance back at her.

"Don't wait for me Strider! Keep going!" she yelled.

He was on the dirt road and past the farm. Again, he glanced back without breaking stride, but Sadie was no longer in sight. The bridge that crossed the Cookes Creek River was around the upcoming curve. Strider had never ventured past the bridge; the area beyond was strictly human territory.

When he rounded the bend, he spotted the truck moving slowly down the rutted road. Strider rushed upon the vehicle and landed in the back of the pickup with a large thud. Startled by the sound, the man stopped the truck.

Grabbing Seth by the scruff of his neck, Strider pulled his son up and out of the box. He leapt back out of the truck and hit the ground running, nearly colliding with Sadie as he rounded the curve in the road.

Strider knew they had to keep running until they were deep into the woods. Once the man realized what had happened, he would probably come looking for them.

Strider and Sadie didn't stop until they reached the clearing. Only then did Strider gently place the puppy on the ground and release him from his jaw. Feeling a bit disoriented, Seth stood up and shook himself off.

"Oh, Seth, thank goodness you're safe!" Sadie exclaimed with relief. Upon hearing his mother's voice, Seth turned and ran to her. She examined him thoroughly as she peppered him with questions. "Are you okay? Did you get hurt? Were you scared?"

Strider stood nearby and watched the two. The warmth of his love for them filled his being. Sadie suddenly realized they hadn't included him in their celebration. She stopped and with great pride said, "Seth, I would like you to meet your father."

Strider walked over to his son and bent his head down to him. "I'm pleased to meet you, Seth." Seth stretched up to his father's face and gave him a kiss with his small pink tongue. Strider kissed him back and a strong paternal love flowed through him.

Sadie and Strider knew the clearing wasn't a safe place to stay, so they decided to retreat to the cave. Seth, recovered from his harrowing experience, scampered about and explored the trail ahead of his parents.

"We should be safe in the cave tonight," Strider said quietly when Seth was momentarily out of earshot. "But we need to leave as soon as we wake up tomorrow to start our journey north. It's too dangerous for us to stay here."

"Seth! Don't go too far ahead!" his mother called out. She turned to Strider. "What are we going to do about Missy? We can't leave without her."

Strider hesitated before he responded. "We have no other choice for now," he said, keeping his voice low. "The danger is too great for either of us to go back to get Missy. She'll be safe until we can come back for her."

Sadie knew Strider was right, but it didn't make leaving Missy any easier. Though Missy liked the farmer's wife and was already popular with the other farm animals, Sadie couldn't keep from worrying. When she finally fell asleep that night, after tossing and turning for hours, her dreams were filled with images of the daughter she was about to leave behind.

Seth woke up the next morning bright and early, eager to start the day. The night before, his parents had told him they were all going on a long journey to live in a new place. Strider stressed to his son how difficult the trip would be, but Seth was so excited he barely heard his father's words.

A short time after waking, the family started their journey. When they came to the top of the ridge that would put the farm behind them, Sadie turned for one last look in its direction. "I love you, Missy," she whispered. "We'll be back. I promise."

CHAPTER 6

THE YEAR PASSED quickly for Sadie and Strider. Seth rapidly grew into the largest and strongest pup of the pack, exhibiting leadership qualities almost as soon as they arrived. Strider hoped one day his son would be the head of the pack as his father had been and his father before him. Strider's heart swelled with pride and love as he stood and watched Seth play with the other pups.

The day had finally arrived for Sadie and Strider to embark on their journey back to the Baileys' farm to fulfill their promise to bring Missy home. Seth would stay with the pack while they were gone, though he had begged his parents to let him go along.

As Strider and Sadie progressed across the miles of landscape that had separated them from their daughter for the past year, their anticipation of seeing Missy grew. At dusk on the seventh day of the journey they arrived at the last ridge of hills that gave way to the lowlands and to the Baileys' farm.

Reluctantly, Sadie agreed to wait at the cave that evening while Strider went to scout out the farm under the cover of darkness. If there was any possibility of retrieving Missy safely, he would do so; otherwise, he would return to the farm each evening at dusk until the opportunity to rescue her arose.

When Strider stepped out of the woods at the perimeter of the farm he immediately knew something was wrong. The scents of the farm he should have detected were absent, and the house and outbuildings sat in dark stillness. There was no evidence of life other than the occasional sound of small creatures scurrying through the overgrown fields and the intermittent calls of night insects. He cautiously made his way across the untended cornfield.

The farm was deserted.

Old scents lingered, some of them Sadie's, but there were no fresh ones here. He warily proceeded to the house where the humans had lived. It also was dark and appeared to be abandoned. No one had lived there recently.

Missy was gone.

Sadie would be heartbroken.

Strider headed back to the cave, his heart heavy with sorrow.

Though neither Sadie nor Strider would ever see Missy again, their legacy would live on through her and her descendants. A legacy that had begun one fateful autumn day, when an unusual friendship was transformed into a story of love and courage that would impact the lives of both dogs and humans alike in the years to come; especially the lives of Toby and Tara.

PART II
TOBY AND TARA

✧　✧　✧

"When the Man waked up he said,
'What is the Wild Dog doing here?'
And the Woman said,
'His name is not Wild Dog any more,
but the First Friend,
because he will be our friend
for always and always and always.'"

– Rudyard Kipling

CHAPTER 7

THE LONG, HOT summer passed by lazily for Toby and Tara. They spent their days playing with the boy or with the other young farm animals. There was Rudy, the piglet, with whom they would only play with outside of the sty; Shelby, one of the resident kittens who had recently begun scratching them during their bouts of play; and Elsa, the goat, who was their best friend and the most fun to play with.

At least once a week they asked their mother to retell the story of their how their Grandma Sadie and Grandpa Strider met, and she always obliged them.

Missy spent her days watching over Toby and Tara when they weren't frolicking about the farm. The rest of her litter had been sold, and she wondered if the farmer planned to sell her two remaining pups. Hopefully, he would decide to keep them, just as he had decided to keep her several years earlier; but she knew hope alone would not grant her wish.

As Toby saw his siblings taken from the farm one by

one, he wondered whether he and Tara would experience the same fate. As the summer progressed the question plagued him more frequently. He didn't want to be taken from the farm, or away from his mother, Tara, and their friends.

One day in late August, Toby ran into the barn where he found his mother resting in the cool darkness of the old building.

"Mama?" he asked, his head characteristically cocked to one side. Missy raised one eyelid.

"Yes, Toby?"

"Are you sleeping?"

"No. I was just resting," she replied. "Is anything wrong?"

"I was just wondering if Tara and I will be taken away to a new home like the others."

Missy sat up. The fear she had been trying to keep from her pups resurfaced. Had Toby sensed her concern? Before she could respond, Toby continued on.

"I don't want to leave the farm, Mama. I like it here. I'd miss my friends and the boy and the farmer's helper," Toby said. "And I never want to leave you and Tara. I want to stay here forever. Okay?" Toby didn't wait for an answer; instead he leaned forward, gave his mother a kiss on the nose, and ran out of the barn to go play with his sister, confident his mother could protect him from the fate of his siblings.

Missy sighed. There was a lot of worrying that went along with being a mother. She laid her head down on her paws and tried to go back to sleep, but the thoughts running through her mind kept her from the rest she sought.

✦ ✦ ✦

MICHAEL SPENT MUCH of his free time that summer playing with Toby and Tara, and that was exactly what he was doing when Walt came out of the barn. He watched with amusement as the puppies pounced on Michael, who was face down on the grass with his arms covering his head. Toby and Tara sniffed and pawed as they tried to get at the boy's face. Their wet noses tickled Michael, and he rolled over laughing.

"You won't be able to call them puppies much longer. They're going to be the size of horses soon," Walt said, as he sat down on the grass next to Michael.

"They're getting big, huh? Especially Little Chief," said Michael.

"Pretty soon we'll have to call him Big Chief," Walt said, and the two of them laughed.

Mr. Bailey walked out of the barn just as Michael and Walt's laughter subsided. Michael's attachment to the dogs had grown, and something needed to be done about the problem soon. All of the other puppies from the litter had been sold. The time had come to get rid of the white ones. He would tell Mrs. Bailey tonight, he decided. In the meantime, Michael needed something better to do with his time.

"Michael!" he yelled to his son.

"What, Dad?" Michael knew his father didn't like to see him playing with the puppies. He always seemed angry when they were together. Michael could tell by the look on his father's face that he was angry now.

"Are you done with your chores?" his father asked.

"Yes, Dad. I finished them earlier."

"Good, because I have something else I need you to do."

"Aww, Dad, do I have to?"

"If you have time to play with those dogs, then you have time to do some more chores around here."

Michael reluctantly got up and spent the remainder of the afternoon cleaning out the horse barn.

That evening, after Michael went to bed, Mr. Bailey brought up the subject of the two puppies to his wife.

"We have to do something about those dogs," Mr. Bailey said after he turned down the radio they were listening to.

"What dogs?" Mrs. Bailey asked distractedly, as she concentrated on following the intricate pattern of a cross-stitch design.

"Those two white puppies," he replied impatiently. "Michael's become way too attached to them. The problem is getting out of hand. He spends all his free time playing with them, and now he has Walt wrapped up in them, too."

Mrs. Bailey stopped what she was doing and turned to look at her husband over the top of her reading glasses; her brown eyes gazed at him steadily.

"If Michael has become attached to the puppies, it's because you waited too long to find them a home," she said, and turned back to her embroidery hoop. "Anyway, I don't see why we can't keep them. Having a couple more dogs on a farm this size wouldn't be unreasonable, and they seem smart and have good dispositions."

But Mr. Bailey was adamant about the two white

puppies; they were not going to stay on the farm no matter how much Michael wanted to keep them, or Mrs. Bailey, for that matter.

"Walt's going to get rid of those dogs tomorrow and that's that," Mr. Bailey declared to his wife.

"What do you mean 'get rid of them'?" she asked, eyeing Mr. Bailey suspiciously.

"I mean get rid of them. Walt can take 'em out to the woods and shoot 'em or drown 'em in the river. I don't care."

Mrs. Bailey, shocked at her husband's suggestion, looked up from her embroidery and said, "I can't believe you'd be so cruel to your son. You could at least try to give them away." Knowing how stubborn and unyielding her husband could be, she knew she wasn't going to win this fight completely, but she hoped she could at least keep the poor puppies from being killed.

"No one wants white German Shepherds, and the older they get, the harder it'll be to get rid of them."

"Can't we take them to the animal shelter?" Mrs. Bailey suggested.

"No," said Mr. Bailey. "Business went down back in Cookes County after I advertised that white abomination of a dog at the post office. I don't want to ruin my reputation here, too."

Mrs. Bailey's heart dropped. Her mind raced.

"Can't we tell Michael that Walt is taking them to the animal shelter? Will you at least agree to that?" Mrs. Bailey asked hopefully.

Mr. Bailey thought for a moment.

"I guess so, but someday he'll have to learn the harsher

facts of life," he said, and leaned over to turn the radio back on.

End of discussion, thought Mrs. Bailey.

That night, while Mrs. Bailey lay in bed, she couldn't stop thinking about the poor little puppies. At two o'clock in the morning, she was still awake. The puppies were so sweet and good-natured. And poor Michael, even if they lied to him about what happened to the puppies, she would still feel horrible about the truth. She rolled over again and tried to find a comfortable position. An hour later, after a lot more thought, she finally fell asleep, knowing exactly what she had to do in the morning.

CHAPTER 8

MRS. BAILEY WOKE up at six the next morning. She slowly got out of bed so as not to wake Mr. Bailey. On weekdays he would have been up by now, but he slept in on Saturdays. Mrs. Bailey quickly threw on a t-shirt and jeans, put on a pair of sneakers, and pulled her hair back into a ponytail. She tiptoed out of the bedroom and quietly slipped out of the house. Walt would be up by now; he was always the first one up.

She walked across the lawn through the dew-soaked grass. The day was going to be another scorcher. The sun hung low and heavy above the horizon. Summer was going out with a bang. Record high temperatures had been hanging around for over a week, and with the high humidity levels, life was miserable for everyone. By the time she arrived at the stable where Walt always started his day, her t-shirt had begun to stick to her back.

Once inside the dark coolness of the horse barn, Mrs. Bailey found Walt in the back rubbing down one of the saddles with an oil rag. She loved the earthy scents of the stable. Having been brought up with horses, she especially liked to go riding early in the morning or at dusk before the sun went down.

"Good morning, Walt," she said softly so as not to startle him.

"Oh, good morning, Mrs. Bailey." Walt greeted her in his usual good-natured way. "What brings you out here so early? Going for a ride?"

"Maybe later. Right now I have something important I want to discuss with you, but I don't want Mr. Bailey or Michael to know about our conversation."

"Sounds serious. What's the matter?"

Mrs. Bailey told Walt the details of her conversation with Mr. Bailey the night before.

"I just can't let those poor puppies be killed," she ended.

"To be honest with you, Mrs. Bailey, I've been expecting something like this. Mr. Bailey hasn't hidden his dislike for those dogs since the day they were born. I'll help you any way I can. Just tell me what you want me to do."

"Thanks, Walt. I knew I could count on you." Mrs. Bailey smiled at him and wondered why Mr. Bailey couldn't have some of Walt's pleasant disposition. "I've been giving this a lot of thought. There's an animal shelter up in Kimball. Mrs. Antarsh, Joey's mother, told me about the place."

"I've heard of that shelter. One of my friends adopted a dog there," Walt said.

"Mrs. Antarsh volunteers at the shelter once a week to help find homes for the animals left there," Mrs. Bailey continued. "I thought I'd call her this morning to see if we could take the puppies there. At least they'd have a chance of getting a good home. What do you think?"

"Sounds like a good idea to me. When Mr. Bailey comes to me about the puppies, I'll tell him I need to go to Willows to run a few personal errands. I'll suggest that I dispose of the dogs in the Aledo Canal on the way into town . . ."

"But instead you'll take the puppies to the animal shelter in Kimball . . ."

"And Mr. Bailey will never know the difference," Walt finished. The plan was set.

A short time later that morning, Mr. Bailey approached Walt in the barn and gave the awaited order to dispose of the puppies. Mr. Bailey liked Walt's idea of drowning the dogs in the canal instead of shooting them. The new plan fit in nicely with the story he had agreed to tell Michael about Walt taking them to his friend's farm. He left Walt, satisfied the problem was taken care of.

✧　✧　✧

TOBY WAS THE FIRST of the farm animals to be up and about most mornings—besides Rusty the rooster—and this morning was no exception. He waited as long as he could for his sister to wake up, but his patience evaporated quickly, and he gently pushed her with his nose until her eyes fluttered open. Tara slowly stretched as she lay there, then stood up without complaint and stretched some more, after which the two of them ran off to visit Elsa the goat.

Elsa loved to play with Toby and Tara, and was the only farm animal with enough energy to keep up with Toby. Tara, as usual, tired out first, and carefully removed herself from the hoopla to watch the fun from the sidelines, cheering her brother on as he play-fought with Elsa. After an hour or so, when the two frolickers finally tired out, Toby and Tara said good-bye to their friend and headed back to the barn to see if their mother was awake.

Missy was able to sleep late now that the puppies were older. A well-deserved privilege, she felt. But today she was restless and rose earlier than usual. She stretched her legs and tried to shake off the small pieces of hay that had stuck to her fur while she slept. She saw that Toby and Tara were already up and gone. Missy knew the two would soon return to tell her all about their morning adventures.

Sunshine poured through the open barn door. Nearby, Rusty, the farm's resident rooster, crowed again. Missy decided to wait outside for her children. As she started toward the door, the farmer's helper rushed inside. He looked around and quickly left again. Missy didn't give the incident much thought as she stepped out of the dark, cool barn into the bright, warm sunshine; after all, the farmer's helper was always going in and out of the barn.

Cookie, a large orange tabby, lay in the grass on the side of the path leading from the barn. Next to her, curled into little orange fur balls, slept Shelby and her three siblings.

"Good morning, Cookie," Missy greeted the tabby. Cookie stretched and opened her mouth wide in a lazy yawn.

"Oh, good morning," she replied, as she rolled into a semi-upright position. "You're up early today. It appears everyone on the farm decided to rise early. Are you in on it, too?"

"In on what?" Missy asked. She knew Cookie liked to gossip and usually didn't give much credence to the rumors the tabby circulated, but today the cat's comments pricked her curiosity.

"I'm not sure, but something's stirring," replied Cookie.

Just then the farmer's helper came around the corner of the barn with Toby in one arm and Tara in the other.

✧ ✧ ✧

WALT WANTED TO give the puppies a chance to say good-bye to their mother before he took them away. He squatted next to Missy just as Cookie ran off, her kittens trailing behind her.

"I want you to say good-bye to your mother before we leave," he said to Toby and Tara, and then turned to Missy. "I know you're going to miss your puppies, but they can't stay here. Mr. Bailey won't allow it. They'll be better off somewhere else. Hopefully the shelter will find a good home for both of them. I know they'll try." Walt waited while Missy and her puppies sniffed each other. After a few moments, he rose and went back to the house where Michael stood on the front porch with his mother waiting to say good-bye to the dogs.

Michael watched Walt approach the house with Toby and Tara in his arms. He tried to be brave, but tears welled up in his eyes. Walt carried the puppies to the bottom of the porch steps. Struggling to hold back his tears, Michael went down to see them one last time.

Michael had let his tears flow freely when his mother told him the puppies were leaving the farm, and she had put her arms around him in consolation. The same tears, Michael knew, would annoy his father who had come out to sit on the porch; crying was for sissies, and his son was not going to behave like a sissy. He sniffed and quickly wiped his eyes with his forearm before he reached out for Toby.

"Come on now," said Mr. Bailey, "let's get the show on the road. Say good-bye and let Walt get going."

Mrs. Bailey turned and gave her husband a sharp look. "Let him have a few minutes. Walt's not in any hurry."

Michael held each puppy one last time and gave them each a kiss on the top of the head. As their soft, white fur brushed his lips, he once again had to fight back the tears. He reluctantly gave the puppies back to Walt, who took them to the truck and placed them in the produce box he had set on the passenger seat. As he secured the lid, one of them began to whimper.

Knowing the sound of the frightened puppy would further upset Michael, Walt hopped in the truck and started the engine. There was no easy way to part a boy from his dogs. Walt had first-hand experience with that and felt bad for his young friend.

As the truck pulled out of the driveway, Michael watched it disappear down the dirt road that led to town.

"Good-bye, Little Chief. Good-bye, White Cloud," he whispered softly. "I'll never forget you." He felt his mother place her arm around his shoulder.

"Come on, Michael. Let's go eat some breakfast. I made your favorite this morning, blueberry pancakes," said Mrs. Bailey, as she gently led Michael up the porch steps.

"Shoot!" Mr. Bailey exclaimed, startling Michael and his mother.

"What's the matter?" Mrs. Bailey asked.

"I forgot to tell Walt to pick up some fertilizer while he was in town. Oh well, I guess I'll go get it myself." He reluctantly pulled himself out of the old wicker rocker. "I haven't taken old Bessie out in a while, and she needs some gas. I'll stop at Milt's on the way to buy the fertilizer. Be back shortly," he said, and left to get Bessie, his 1957 red Chevy Impala, out of the garage.

✧ ✧ ✧

WHEN MISSY HEARD the muffled cries of her puppies coming from inside the large black pickup truck, she reacted instinctively and ran toward the sound. But she was too late. The truck was moving down the driveway toward the dirt road to town. Missy's puppies were following a destiny that had been played out before; but this time Strider was not there to rescue them.

CHAPTER 9

THE TRUCK BOUNCED along the bumps and ruts in the dirt road that led into town. Toby and Tara, petrified by the unexpected turn of events, huddled together in a corner of the box. Several times Toby tried to peer through one of the holes to see where they were going, but each time a jarring jolt thwarted his attempts.

The truck hit another bump.

Tara cried out.

"It's okay," Toby assured her. "The farmer's helper won't hurt us. He's always been nice to us." Toby knew he had to keep up a brave front for his sister, even though inside he was as scared as she was. He had always trusted the farmer's helper before, but now he wondered if his trust was misplaced.

The bouncing suddenly subsided, but the truck continued moving forward. Toby tried to look out one of the holes again, and this time his effort was rewarded. Peering about, he saw some of the inside of the vehicle and a piece of bright blue sky through the window. As he continued to peek through the opening, he was suddenly thrown down again as the truck went over another bump and came to a stop.

Tara cried out again.

The inside of the box was too dark for Toby to see his sister clearly. In the little bit of light that entered through the holes, she was just a ghostly outline huddled in the corner.

✧   ✧   ✧

THE HIGHWAY CUT through the valley that stretched between the distant mountain ranges on either side. Steve Patterson pressed down on the accelerator of his prized Ford Mustang convertible. Even though only four hours had passed since he and his wife Sharon had packed up the campsite at five that morning, Steve felt like he had been driving for days. His eyes were tired and his back hurt. He sat up in the driver's seat. A cup of hot coffee would be good right about now, he thought, and decided to get off the highway at the next exit.

Their week in the Cascades had been spectacular and they still had another week of vacation left. Sharon's sister Lisa and her family planned to visit them for several days on their trip cross-country. Thankfully, they would be staying in a motel since the trailer he and Sharon rented was barely large enough for two, never mind six.

Steve liked Lisa. She reminded him a lot of Sharon. And the two children, Jessica and Justin, were well-behaved. He liked Ray, too, since he had stopped drinking several years ago. In the past, Steve had dreaded their visits. Inevitably, the bottle would come out and Dr. Jekyll would turn into

Mr. Hyde. Then there had been the incident with Drake, the family dog. For Lisa and the kids' sake, Steve hoped Ray had stopped drinking for good this time.

A large green sign loomed up on the side of the road. The next exit was only a mile away in a town called Paradise. Sharon, who had been sleeping in the back seat, began to stir.

"Rise and shine," he called out, looking for her in the rearview mirror. "We're getting off the highway at the next exit. The car needs some gas and I need some coffee. Besides, it's your turn to drive for a while, okay?"

"Okay," Sharon replied sleepily. She sat up and tried to stretch in the tight confines of the Mustang's back seat.

"What time is it?" she asked.

"It's nine o'clock. Did you have a good rest?"

"Yeah," she replied. "It's a little cramped back here, though. It'll be nice to get out of the car."

"Here's the exit now," Steve said, and put on the direction signal.

At the end of the ramp a sign with a symbol of a gasoline pump pointed to the left. Steve took the turn. A large Texaco sign stood on the corner of the upcoming intersection with a smaller white sign that read 'Milt's Garage' perched atop. The light at the intersection was red as Steve pulled up to it behind a black pickup truck.

"We made it," Steve said, and flashed a quick smile in the mirror at his wife. The light turned green and he followed the pickup into the gas station.

With the canal five miles behind him, the plan had worked smoothly so far. One of the puppies, the female, Walt suspected, had been whimpering ever since they left the farm.

"It's okay, don't cry. You're going to have a new home soon," he cooed.

The truck needed gas to make it to Kimball, and Milt's was the only gas station around for miles. Walt looked in the rearview mirror while he waited at a red light before the turn into Milt's driveway. A black Ford Mustang convertible came to a stop behind him.

The light turned green.

The Mustang followed Walt into Milt's.

Walt pulled up to the gas pumps and shut off the truck's engine. The Mustang pulled up on the other side. A man, close to Walt's age, stepped out of the car. Walt jumped down out of the truck and nodded to the man.

"Nice car," Walt said with admiration once he had the pump operating. "What year is it?" The car was in mint condition, no dents or rust.

"Thanks. It's a '65," Steve replied proudly. A woman sat in the backseat. She smiled at Walt; he smiled back.

"That was a good year for Mustangs," observed Walt. "I always dreamed of having a Mustang convertible when I was a teenager, but when I finally could afford one, I got a truck instead; more practical in these parts."

"We probably should have been more practical. It's kind of small for camping trips," Steve said. After a moment, the gas nozzle in his hand clicked, indicating the tank was full. Another car waited in line for the pump.

"It's a beauty," Walt said.

"Thanks," Steve said, and got into the car.

"I'll pull over next to that dumpster, go pay for the gas

and get us some coffee," he said to his wife, who was still in the back seat.

"Good," said Sharon. "I'll use the bathroom and clean out the car while you do that."

Walt watched the Mustang pull away from the pumps and park beside the building. He turned back and continued pumping. While he waited for the click of the nozzle, Walt glanced up at the road. A red car was stopped at the intersection.

"Oh, no!" Walt exclaimed. The car was Mr. Bailey's, he was sure of that. There was no mistaking a bright red 1957 Chevy Impala; it was one of a kind. The right signal light was on. Mr. Bailey was going to pull into Milt's!

Walt's body went into action before his mind had time to think. He released the gas pump and opened the passenger side door. He grabbed the box containing the puppies. Walking as fast as he could with his precious cargo, he headed toward the dumpster where the now empty black Mustang was parked.

Walt couldn't let Mr. Bailey find out he hadn't drowned the puppies or he'd probably be fired. For all Mr. Bailey's faults—and Walt had experienced most of them—he preferred working for him over many of the other bosses he had worked for in the past.

Walt quickly placed the box on the ground next to the dumpster and rushed back to where Mr. Bailey now waited for him next the to truck.

He saw me with the box, Walt thought.

"Hey, Walt!" Mr. Bailey shouted. "Fancy meeting you here. What were you doing over there?"

"Hey, Mr. Bailey." Walt was shaken by the unexpectedness of the encounter. "I needed some gas and thought I'd stop off here at Milt's before heading to Kimball."

"No, I mean what were you doing over by the dumpster with that box? Isn't that the box those dogs were in?"

"Oh, I . . . I was just throwing away some junk I had in the back of the pick-up. I'm surprised to see you here with old Bessie. You haven't had her out in a long time." Walt hoped he had successfully changed the subject.

"I forgot to tell you to pick up some fertilizer . . ." Mr. Bailey continued talking but Walt no longer heard him. The woman from the black Mustang came out of the restroom. The box containing the puppies sat on the ground only a few yards away.

"Walt," said Mr. Bailey. "I said did you take care of dogs? I assume everything went as planned."

Walt tore his attention away from the dumpster and looked blankly at Mr. Bailey.

"Oh, yeah. Fine. Everything went fine."

"Good. I'm glad that's done with."

Walt's attention drifted back to the dumpster, where he saw the woman throwing away a bag of garbage.

TOBY LOST HIS balance and fell against Tara as the box rose and moved back and forth with the rhythm of the man's quick strides. A moment later, the box dropped and landed on the ground. Toby felt his insides rush up into his throat.

Tara cried out.

Then all was still.

Toby's heart pounded in his ears. His sister lay against

him, soft whimpering sounds rose from where her head was buried in his side. He remained motionless for a moment, listening. The sounds around them were distant and muted. Toby slowly sat up.

"Are you okay, Tara?"

"Is it over?" she asked.

"I'm not sure," Toby replied. "Are you hurt?"

"No, I'm just scared. What happened?"

"I don't know, but we're not in the truck anymore. I'll try to see where we are."

Toby peered out of the nearest hole and looked around. He moved from hole to hole. He suddenly stopped. Directly in front of them, about fifty feet away, stood the farmer! He was talking to the farm hand. What's going on? Toby wondered. A multitude of scents wafted into the box as he watched the two men. He jumped up and stuck his nose out one of the upper holes. His head hit the top of the box causing the lid to shift slightly upward.

"Look!" Toby said. "The top of the box moved when my head hit it. Maybe if I keep jumping, I can push the lid off." He wasn't sure how they would get out of the box after that, but he would think of something.

"Do you think it will work?" Tara asked.

"It can't hurt to try."

Toby jumped up over and over again. Each time the lid moved a little more. A crack of light appeared. Toby stopped for a moment to rest. The temperature inside the box was rising from the heat of the sun's rays. He took a deep breath and began jumping again.

CHAPTER 10

STEVE PARKED THE car next to the dumpster.

Sharon climbed out of the back seat and stood next to the car. She arched her back to stretch out the kinks from the long drive.

"I'll be right back," Steve said, as he disappeared around the corner of the building.

Once inside the gas station, Steve looked around for coffee. The place had a couple of old vending machines for candy and soda and a few racks with mostly staples on them: bread, toilet paper, canned goods. He spotted a coffee maker on the counter next to the register. The elderly man reading a newspaper behind the counter appeared to be the only one there. He looked up as Steve approached.

"Hi, there. How are you doing this morning?" the man asked.

Sharon used the restroom and went back to the car. She grabbed a plastic bag from out of the trunk and proceeded to pick up the trash from the floor of the front and back seat. Once done, she carried the bag over to the dumpster and heaved it over the rim. As she turned to go back to the car, a loud yelp came from the other side of the dumpster.

THE SOUND OF footsteps approached, and a shadow passed over the box, momentarily blocking the light. The footsteps receded.

Bang!

A door slammed shut.

All was quiet again.

"What was that?" Tara asked.

"I don't know. But if we hear someone again, I'm going to try to get their attention."

"I hope someone helps us."

"Someone will," Toby assured her. He hoped he was right and resumed working on the lid.

Bang!

Footsteps approached again. Another shadow moved over the box, and though Toby panted heavily from his exertions, he took a deep breath and yelped as loud as he could. This time his efforts were rewarded. The lid of the box was lifted off and the world filled with light.

✧   ✧   ✧

THE YELP SOUNDED like a hurt dog. Sharon hurried to the other side of the dumpster. When she rounded the corner, she almost stumbled over a large crate-like box on the ground. The lid was tilted. She reached forward and lifted it. Two white puppies blinked up at her.

"Well!" she exclaimed. "Look at you two." She reached into the box and gently picked up Toby just as Steve came back with the coffee. He looked at Sharon and the puppy in surprise.

"What have you got there?" he asked.

"Isn't he beautiful?" Sharon asked, as she stroked the soft, white fur. "There are two of them."

"Someone just left them here?" Steve asked.

"I don't know," Sharon replied. "I heard a yelp and found this box sitting here with the puppies in it."

"Why would anyone leave puppies in a box beside a dumpster?"

The same question was on Sharon's mind.

"Did you hear me, Walt?"

"Huh?" Walt replied, once again forcing his attention back to Mr. Bailey.

"I said, you might as well get the fertilizer we need since you have the truck, and I'll take old Bessie back home."

"Oh, okay," Walt said, distracted by the activity at the dumpster. The woman now leaned over the box. Walt watched as she lifted the lid off. He had heard the yelp that had drawn her to the box. He was certain Mr. Bailey heard it, too. But his boss had continued talking without skipping a beat, too involved with what he was saying to notice the sound.

"Are you okay, Walt? You seem kind of out of it."

"I'm fine, Mr. Bailey," he answered. "Just a little tired, that's all. I got up earlier than usual today." Walt glanced back toward the dumpster. The woman cradled one of the puppies in her arms.

"Well, I'll see you back at the farm," Mr. Bailey said, still oblivious to the drama unfolding. "Can you move your truck so I can fill Bessie up? I'll pay Milt for your gas. You go on and do what you have to do. I'll see you later."

"Okay, Mr. Bailey," Walt said, as his gaze nervously shifted to the dumpster and back.

A large camper had pulled up to the pump on the other side of the small island, blocking the view of the dumpster from Mr. Bailey's line of sight. Walt climbed into the truck and pulled away. In the rearview mirror, he could see Mr. Bailey pull Bessie into the spot he had just vacated. Hopefully, Mr. Bailey would pay for the gas and leave without taking time to chat with Milt. Whatever happened now was out of Walt's control.

"Do you think someone wanted to get rid of them?" Sharon asked Steve, as she continued to stroke Toby's head.

"Why else would someone have left them here in this box? It must have felt like an oven in there with this hot sun. They're lucky we came along."

Steve reached in to pet Tara, but she shrank back from his hand.

"This one seems scared, poor thing."

"Maybe whoever left them here hoped someone would find them and give them a home," Sharon suggested.

"There are better ways to find dogs a home," Steve said

with disgust. "Let's get them some water from the thermos. They must be thirsty. They're panting pretty heavily."

Sharon placed Toby back in the box. Steve looked at the two puppies huddled together as he carried the box to the car.

"Don't worry, I'm not going to hurt you," Steve assured them, and carefully carried the box over to the Mustang. Halfway there, he spotted a bright red car out of the corner of his eye. An old red Chevy Impala pulled out of the gas station.

Steve gave a long, low whistle. "What a beauty," he remarked as the car drove off. A large camper and a small green pick-up followed the Impala out of the driveway. Steve set the box on the ground next to the car

"I'll go see if this Milt guy knows anything about the puppies. Be right back." Steve turned and disappeared around the corner of the building.

"Okay," said Sharon, only halfway hearing him as she began to occupy herself with getting the puppies to drink some water. "Come on, little guys. It's okay, don't be scared," she cooed tenderly. Toby leaned toward the offered cup and tentatively lapped the water.

Steve came back from around the corner. "You're not going to believe this, but that guy Milt is gone and the place is locked up. There's not a soul here. He left a note saying he'd be back at 10:30."

"But it's only 9:30," Sharon said.

"I know. What are we going to do now?"

Sharon needed only a moment to think. "Let's take them with us, Steve."

"We can't have dogs right now," said Steve. "We could

be transferred again at any time. It wouldn't be fair to them."

"I don't mean to keep them. We can find them a home. A lot of people in our trailer park have dogs. We'd only have them for a short time. Besides, what else can we do? We can't leave them here."

"I know, but . . ."

Sharon knew Steve would relent; it was the only thing they could do. He loved animals and had always had dogs when he was growing up.

Steve gave in. "Okay, I don't see what other choice we have."

Sharon went over and gave her husband a big hug.

"Don't worry," she reassured him. "Finding a home for them won't take long. They're beautiful animals and they seem healthy. They must have been well taken care of before this. Do you think they're purebred German Shepherds?"

"I don't know," said Steve, as he bent down over the box. "I've never seen purebred white German Shepherds before, but I doubt anyone would get rid of purebred puppies. They'd be worth some money."

"That's true. Anyway, when we get home we should take them to a vet to make sure they're okay. Maybe the vet will be able to tell us what kind of dogs they are."

Steve scratched the top of Toby's head. Tara was still huddled in the corner.

"We'd better get going if we want to get home in time for your sister's arrival," said Steve. He placed the box on the back seat of the car. "I think I'll sit in the back and keep them company for now."

A short distance from Milt's, Walt pulled off the main road into an empty parking lot. Five minutes should be enough time for Mr. Bailey to leave the gas station, he thought.

He tapped his fingers on the dashboard as the seconds ticked by, impatiently watching the clock in his truck. What would he find when he got back to the gas station? He decided to wait an extra minute and then left his hideout.

Walt pulled into Milt's. A "Closed" sign hung on the front door. Milt must have gone out for something, he thought, and pulled around to the side of the building where the dumpster was located. The box and the black Mustang were gone.

"Oh, no!" he exclaimed. His mind began to race. Did the young couple take the puppies? Did Mr. Bailey see the couple with the dogs and take them himself? If he had, Walt might be out of a job now, and worse, the puppies might be dead. He prayed the young couple had taken them.

Walt briefly considered trying to catch up to the Mustang, but dismissed the idea. They'd be too far away by now. He knew he'd have to tell Mrs. Bailey what happened; she'd eventually find out from her friend at the shelter that the puppies had never arrived. All he could do was hope for the best.

✧ ✧ ✧

TOBY AND TARA FOUND themselves back in the box—this time with the lid off—inside another vehicle with the man and woman who had found them. The man had gotten in the back seat with them and was petting Toby's head.

"I think they're going to help us," Toby said to his sister in a low voice.

"I hope so," Tara whispered. "I'm getting awfully hungry. I miss Mama, too. Do you think they'll take us back home?"

"We'll have to wait and see," Toby replied, but he had a terrible feeling they would never see their mother, or the farm, again.

PART III
ON THE ROAD

✧   ✧   ✧

"Our task must be to free ourselves...
By widening our circle of compassion
to embrace all living creatures
and the whole of nature and its beauty."

– Albert Einstein

CHAPTER 11

STEVE PULLED THE Mustang into the narrow gravel driveway next to their trailer. Sharon peered over the back of the passenger seat into the box. Both puppies were sleeping. She reached back and gently stroked the top of Tara's head. The puppy woke up with a start and scrunched herself back into the corner of the box. Sharon pulled her hand away.

"How are the puppies doing?" Steve asked, as he turned off the engine.

"Good. They're just waking up."

"Let's get them settled in before your sister and the kids arrive." Steve climbed out of the car and removed the box from the back seat while Sharon unlocked the trailer.

"Where should I put them?" Steve asked.

"Put them in the living room for now."

Steve took the puppies inside and placed the box on the floor next to the couch. Sharon followed behind Steve with an armload of stuff from the car and set the pile down on the kitchen table. The message indicator on the answering machine blinked. She pressed the play button.

"Hi, Sharon! Hi, Steve! It's Lisa. I hope you're not rushing home to meet us. Ray wanted to stay in Vegas a little longer to do some golfing, so we're going straight to the motel tonight instead of stopping by to see you. Ray still wants to go golfing with Steve tomorrow, so you and I can take the kids to the beach after lunch like we planned. We'll be at your place around eleven tomorrow morning. If that's a problem, call me. Can't wait to see you. Love you both." The message shut off just as Steve came through the door with the last of the camping equipment.

"Was that Lisa?"

"Yeah, they're not coming over until tomorrow morning. They'll be here around eleven. Ray wanted to spend a little more time in Las Vegas to play golf."

"Good. I'm beat."

"Me, too," Sharon concurred. "He still wants to go golfing with you tomorrow. Okay?"

"Yeah, I'm looking forward to it. He's a pretty good golfer."

She went over to Steve, gave him a quick kiss on the cheek, and then said, "I'm glad you and Ray are getting along now that he's not drinking. Why don't you take the dogs out to go to the bathroom while I start putting some of this stuff away."

Steve took Toby and Tara outside. After a moment, Sharon heard the next door neighbors' dog barking. She had forgotten about Max, the Wright's Doberman Pinscher.

"We'd better keep those puppies away from Max," she said to Steve when he came back in with the dogs.

"I don't think Max would hurt them. He's a good-natured

dog. Besides, he's always tethered when he's outside." He gently placed the puppies back in the box. "While I was out there, I was thinking I could put up a temporary pen for these little guys tomorrow morning by using the leftover chicken wire we have from the fence we put around the garden. Where are they going to sleep tonight?"

"I think we should just put a towel in the box and keep them right where they are. The box is familiar to them. They probably think of it as their home, or at least their home away from home," Sharon replied.

"I'll put a small bowl of water in the corner for them," Steve said.

"Good idea. Then let's go out and get something to eat before I pass out from hunger. After that, we can stop at the grocery store and buy some dog food."

"Do you think the puppies will be okay by themselves?" Steve asked.

"Sure," Sharon said. "We'll leave a light on for them. They'll be fine."

TOBY STOOD UP and peered out of the box. The dim light from a small lamp cast a soft glow over the room. The repetitive ticking of a clock in another room was the only audible sound.

"I hope they're not going to leave us here by ourselves," said Tara.

"They won't. Why would they have taken us with them and been so nice to us if they were going to leave us by ourselves?"

"I guess you're right," she said, and curled up in a corner of the box. Within minutes, she was asleep.

Toby hoped he could stay awake until the man and woman came back, but an hour later, when the trailer door opened, he was sound asleep.

CHAPTER 12

THE LAST OF THE morning dew, untouched yet by the sun, clung to the blades of grass that brushed against Toby's legs as he explored the perimeter of the pen. He stopped to push his nose through one of the many small openings in the fence. Tara stopped next to him. A multitude of scents mixed and mingled in the light breeze. He concentrated on identifying them, but most were unfamiliar.

For the most part, the area was quiet. Occasionally a car would go by, drowning out the intermittent sounds of birds and the light rustling of nearby sycamore and cottonwood leaves. With each new sound, Toby stopped and tilted his head, listening carefully. Some sounds were more interesting than others. A door slammed on the other side of the building next door. After a few moments, the scent of another dog pervaded the air.

"Do you smell that?" Toby asked his sister.

"Smell what?"

"That dog scent."

"No . . . oh, yes, now I do. Maybe that's the same dog we heard last night."

"Maybe; the scent is coming from that direction," Toby said.

After a moment, with a note of homesickness in her voice, Tara asked, "Do you think we'll ever see Mama again?"

Toby didn't want to crush Tara's hopes, but he needed to be honest with her.

"The farm is a long way from here, Tara. Remember how long we traveled in the car. And don't forget, we slept during much of the trip. We don't know how far we are from home."

"I know," Tara said, looking down at the ground. "I just wish we could see her again."

The sad look on his sister's face broke Toby's heart.

"Come on, let's keep exploring."

"Okay," Tara replied, and half-heartedly followed her brother.

After thoroughly inspecting their surroundings, the two puppies laid down next to each other to rest in the warm rays of the sun that had crested over the trees. They had just fallen asleep when they were awakened by the barking of the dog next door and the crunching of tires on the gravel driveway.

✧ ✧ ✧

RAY DROVE DOWN the long, winding road that led to the small trailer park.

"Dad," Justin called from the back seat, "how much

longer until we're there?" His mother had let it slip earlier that they were going to the beach that afternoon with his Aunt Sharon while his Uncle Steve and his father went golfing. A beach with big waves. Not like the beaches back home in Connecticut where you were lucky if a ripple from a boat came to shore and the water was always freezing. They were going to a *real* beach.

"If I have the directions right, we should be at your Aunt Sharon's any minute. There it is. Pleasant View Trailer Park." Ray turned into the main entrance. His sister-in-law's trailer was the second trailer on the left.

"There's Aunt Sharon!" Justin cried out. Sharon stood at the end of the driveway waving as they approached; she held something white in her other arm.

"What is she holding?" he asked.

"I can't tell from here," his mother replied.

"Where is she? I can't see her," Jessica said, as she peered out the back window.

"You can't see her from your side. She's on this side," said her father.

As Ray pulled the car into the driveway, Justin cried out, "It's a puppy! She's holding a white puppy!"

"Where? Where? I can't see the puppy," Jessica said, as she strained against the seatbelt. She unhooked the buckle and leaned toward Justin to look out his window. Justin leaned back in his seat.

"See. She's holding a puppy in her arms," he said.

"Oh, it's so cute!" Jessica exclaimed.

Justin had always wanted a puppy. Their dog Drake was rescued by his parents before Justin was born, but Drake was thirteen now and no longer had the energy or ability to play with Justin the way he used to. Even so, Justin loved him as much as ever. His parents had told him that maybe sometime this year they might get him a puppy. Justin hoped it would be a Christmas present. His eleventh birthday had recently passed.

Now he clearly saw the white puppy cradled in his aunt's arm. It looked so small and cute. Justin tried to remain calm, but as soon as the car came to a stop, he jumped out and ran to her.

"Aunt Sharon, you have a puppy!"

"Justin, look how tall you've grown!" Sharon exclaimed. "Give me a big hug and kiss before you grow so tall I can't reach you anymore." She leaned down and gave Justin a squeeze with her free arm. He gave her a kiss on the cheek. Sharon stood back and looked him over. He looked more and more like his father each time she saw him, with the same brown hair and brown eyes. And now that his face was maturing, the resemblance was even stronger.

"What's his name? Can I hold him? Is it a boy puppy?" Justin barraged his aunt with questions.

"*He* doesn't have a name yet, and yes, you may hold him." Justin gently took Toby from Sharon's arms. Jessica ran up to them.

"Hi, Aunt Sharon!" Jessica threw her arms around her aunt's waist. Sharon picked her up and gave her a big hug.

"Can I have a turn to hold the puppy, too?"

"Of course you can, honey," Sharon said, and set Jessica down.

"Can I have a turn for a hug?" It was Lisa.

Ray watched as Lisa and Sharon exchanged greetings. Just then, Steve came around the side of the trailer with another white puppy in the crook of his arm.

"Well now, who would like to hold this puppy for me so I can give everybody a proper hello?" he asked, as he walked toward the group.

"I would! I would! May I hold the puppy, Uncle Steve, please?" Jessica implored.

"Actually, you're exactly who I had in mind for the job. But I need a proper hello first." Steve bent down slightly. Jessica stood on her toes and gave her uncle a kiss on the cheek. He placed Tara in her arms.

"Is it a girl puppy?"

"Yes, ma'am," Steve replied.

"She's so soft," Jessica said, as she held Tara close and kissed the top of her head.

"Mommy, look. Uncle Steve let me hold a puppy, too. It looks just like the one Justin has but it's smaller, and it's a girl. Isn't she cute?"

"My goodness, two puppies?" Lisa looked at Sharon.

"Don't worry. We're not keeping them. We found them on our trip home. They were abandoned. I'll tell you the story later. Meanwhile, the guys need to take off for the golf course. They're meeting two of Steve's friends there for a noon tee-off. I'd better remind them."

"So are you ready to hit some golf balls?" Sharon heard Steve ask Ray as she approached them.

"You bet," Ray replied.

"Hi, Ray!" Sharon greeted her brother-in-law and gave him a quick hug. "Have you been enjoying your trip?"

"It's been great. How was your trip to Oregon?"

"Wonderful, though a little cool at times," Sharon replied. "We'll have to show you some of the pictures we took. But right now, you two better get ready to leave or you'll miss your tee time."

After the two men left, Sharon, Lisa, and the kids went into the trailer to eat lunch and get ready for their trip to the beach. Justin and Jessica played with the puppies on the living room floor.

"Aunt Sharon, will you tell us how you found the puppies?" He was anxious to hear the story.

"Yes, Auntie Sharon, tell us, please?" Jessica chimed in.

"Okay, but first I need to know what kind of sandwiches you want for lunch. I think I have something you both might like. Can you guess what?"

"Peanut butter and Fluff!" the two children cried out at the same time.

"How did you know?" Sharon feigned surprise.

"Because that's our favorite," said Jessica.

"Two peanut butter and Fluff sandwiches coming right up."

"Will you tell us the story *now*?" Justin asked again. Sharon acceded and while she made them all lunch, told the attentive listeners how the puppies came into their care.

"Now we need to find them a good home," she said, as she stuck the knife in the peanut butter jar.

Justin turned to his mother.

"Can't *we* give them a home, Ma? You and Dad said I might be able to get a puppy this year."

"Can we, Mommy?" Jessica joined in. "Justin can have the boy puppy, and I can have the girl puppy!"

"Wait a minute now, kids. I don't know if your father would like the idea of having two puppies in the house."

"We can just take the boy puppy," Justin suggested. "Then Aunt Sharon and Uncle Steve would only have one puppy to find a home for."

"That's not fair," said Jessica through pouting lips. "If Justin can have a puppy, why can't I?"

Lisa looked over at Sharon helplessly.

"Sorry, Sis," Sharon said. "I didn't mean to start any trouble."

"Let's drop the subject for now," Lisa told the kids. "I'll talk to your father about it later."

"Do you think he'll say yes?" Justin asked.

"I don't know, but I wouldn't get my hopes up too high if I were you. Having two puppies is a lot of work. Eat up now, so we can go to the beach."

"The big wave beach," Justin reminded his sister.

"I don't know how big the waves will be today," said Sharon. "But they'll definitely be bigger than the ones back in Connecticut. If they're too big, one of us will have to go into the water with you." She set the plates of sandwiches on the table in the small dining area attached to the living room. The table was only big enough for two.

"Here's your lunch. I'll get you both some milk."

"The big wave beach sounds scary," said Jessica between bites.

"There's nothing to be afraid of," Sharon reassured her, placing the two milks in front of them. "You have to be careful, that's all."

Toby, who had been sleeping on the living room rug next to his sister, stretched and walked over to where Justin sat. Justin reached down to stroke his fur. Toby looked up at him with his head cocked to the side.

"What are you going to name the puppies?" Justin asked.

"We didn't think we should name them since we're not going to keep them. We thought their new owners should name them."

"But they should at least have temporary names, so we can call them something," Justin insisted, and leaned down to pet Toby again. Toby began to sniff and lick Justin's fingers where marshmallow had stuck to them.

"Look! He likes marshmallow! He's licking it off my fingers!"

"Don't let him lick your fingers while you're eating," Lisa admonished her son. "Go wash your hands in the bathroom, then finish your lunch."

"Aww, Ma."

"Come on. Go wash up."

Justin went to the bathroom to wash his hands. When he came back, he walked into the kitchen with a look of revelation on his face.

"I know what we can call the puppies, Marshmallow and Fluff! We can call the boy puppy Marshmallow and the girl puppy Fluff. The names are perfect. They're both white and look like marshmallow fluff." Justin was thrilled with his idea.

"I don't like the name Fluff," Jessica said.

"What about Fluffy then?" her brother suggested.

"I like Fluffy!"

"Can we call them Marshmallow and Fluffy, Aunt Sharon?"

Sharon looked over at their mother, who raised her eyebrows, shrugged her shoulders, and gave her an 'it's up to you' look.

"Okay. We'll call them Marshmallow and Fluffy for now," Sharon agreed. "Now you two finish up your lunch so we can get going." Twenty minutes later they left Toby and Tara sleeping soundly in their box and were on the way to the beach.

✧　✧　✧

TOBY CIRCLED AND lay down in the corner of the box across from where Tara was curled up already asleep. He closed his eyes and his thoughts drifted to his mother. Would they ever see her again? He hoped so, though with each day that passed, the possibility seemed less likely.

Was this going to be their new home? At least Tara was with him; his other siblings had been taken from the farm one at a time; alone. He didn't want to think about being without his sister. She depended on him and her dependence gave him purpose and the strength to get through each day.

Living here wouldn't be so bad, thought Toby. The man and woman treated them well and gave them good food, and the boy and girl were fun to play with. But he knew however much he liked these new humans, they could never take the place of his mother or the farm; this would never be his real home.

CHAPTER 13

LATER THAT AFTERNOON Sharon, Lisa, and the kids—all sunburned and sticky from their day at the beach—arrived back at the trailer park. Steve and Ray sat in lounge chairs next to the puppies' pen. As soon as the car came to a stop, Justin and Jessica jumped out and ran over to their father.

"Dad!" Justin cried out as he ran. "You should've seen the big waves at the beach. They were taller than me!"

"Me, too!" Jessica exclaimed, and gave her father a salty hug and kiss.

"Tell me all about it," said Ray.

"Can we later, Dad? I want to go see Marshmallow first," Justin said, anxious to see the puppy.

"And I want to see Fluffy!" Jessica said excitedly.

"Fluffy? Marshmallow?" Ray looked at the two children and then at Lisa and Sharon.

"Aunt Sarah let us name the puppies!" Jessica exclaimed. "Fluffy is mine and Marshmallow is Justin's."

Sharon shrugged her shoulders and said with a wry smile, "I was outvoted."

As Steve and Ray talked about their day of golfing, Lisa watched Justin and Jessica play with the puppies. On the way back from the beach all the kids had talked about were the puppies. She'd have to broach the subject with Ray later that night.

"The kids are crazy about the puppies," Steve said. "Do you think Ray will agree to let them keep them?"

"I don't know," Sharon replied, and adjusted her head in the crook of Steve's arm as they lay in bed together later that evening. "Even though they told Justin he could get a dog this year, Jessica would be devastated if they only took Marshmallow, and two puppies are a lot of work. The kids keep promising Lisa they'll take care of them, but . . ."

Sharon was silent for a moment.

"What's wrong?" Steve asked.

"I was just thinking about what Ray did to Drake when he was a puppy."

"That was years ago Sharon, when Ray was drinking," Steve reminded her. "In fact, from what I remember, he had gone on a real bender the night it happened."

"I know, but how do we know he won't start drinking again someday?"

"We don't. I guess it's a chance we'd have to take. Besides, it'll be a moot point if he says no. And if he says yes, how can we say no?"

"True. We couldn't say no," Sharon said, as she rolled over to turn out the light on the nightstand. "Jessica and Justin would be devastated."

The golf ball soared through the air in a slow arc, straight and true, slowly gaining altitude before gently descending back to earth. The small white object landed on the putting green inches from the cup, two-hundred and fifty yards from where Steve stood at the tee. The crowd cheered and a telephone began to ring. Who's calling me here? Steve asked himself. The telephone rang again, and he found himself rudely awakened from his dream by the jarring movement of the bed as Sharon jumped up and ran to the kitchen to answer the phone.

"Hello?"

"Sharon, it's Lisa. I hope I didn't wake you."

"Uh . . . nope. We were just getting up. What time is it?"

"It's eight-thirty. You're not going to believe this!"

"What?" Sharon asked, her curiosity pricked by the excitement in her sister's voice.

"Last night Ray and I decided to let the kids have the puppies!"

"That's great!" said Sharon, genuinely surprised and pleased, her concerns from the night before vanquished in the daylight. "Have you told the kids yet?"

"Yes, and they're driving us crazy. They want to come over and see them now, but I told them they have to wait until later when we come over for the cookout. At their insistence, I'm calling to make sure you don't give the puppies away before we get there!"

Sharon laughed. "I can imagine how excited they are," she said. "Steve will be glad to know we won't have to find them a home. He was worried about how long it would take us. Little did we know. . ."

"Listen," said Lisa, "I'll let you go so you can wake up. We'll still be over around eleven. We're going out to breakfast this morning. Then we're going to find a pet store to buy a carrier for the drive back to Connecticut, and the kids want to buy the puppies a couple of toys. Is there anything you need for the cookout?"

"Nope. I think we're all set. Just bring yourselves," said Sharon.

"Okay. We'll see you later then."

"Bye, Sis." Sharon hung up the telephone, started the coffee-maker, and went back to the bedroom.

"Was that Lisa?" Steve asked, as Sharon slipped back into bed for a few more minutes of rest while the coffee brewed.

"Yeah, and guess what? Ray decided to let the kids have the puppies!"

"That's great! Justin and Jessica must be ecstatic."

"They are," replied Sharon. "They were worried we were going to give the dogs away before they got here today."

Steve laughed and said, "I'm glad the puppies will be able to stay together. The female never leaves her brother's side."

The pleasant aroma of fresh-brewed coffee drifted into the bedroom.

"Time to rise and shine, mister," Sharon said, as she pulled the covers off her husband. "I have to make potato salad this morning for the cookout, and you need to get the grill out and clean it up. It's been a while since we've used it."

"Yes, ma'am." Steve saluted her.

"And while I pour the coffee, you can take Marshmallow and Fluffy out to go to the bathroom." Steve groaned and rolled out of bed.

Justin and Jessica sat in the restaurant anxiously waiting for their parents to finish their breakfast. Justin, having long since finished his pancakes, dragged his finger through the maple syrup remaining on his plate and popped the sticky digit in his mouth, quickly pulling it through his pursed lips, creating a soft popping sound. Next to him, Jessica had eaten most of her French toast and pushed the last piece around the plate with her fork, creating designs in the syrup. Both children shifted anxiously in their seats.

"You two are acting like you have ants in your pants," said their father.

"We can't help it, Dad," said Justin. "We can't wait to go to Aunt Sharon's to see the puppies. I miss Marshmallow already."

"Me, too," Jessica chimed in. "I can't wait to see Fluffy. She's so soft and cute."

"I hope you both feel that way when they get older," their mother said. "Dogs are a big responsibility, and you'll both have to keep your end of the bargain to help take care of them."

"We'll take care of them, Ma, and we won't forget about Drake either. Right, Jessica?" Justin looked at his sister.

"Right. We're going to take the best care of all of them," Jessica stated with absolute certainty.

On the way to the pet store the motel owner had

directed them to, Ray thought about his decision to let the kids have the puppies. When he had seen the puppies at his sister-in-law's, he knew the kids would ask if they could have them. Justin had been asking for a puppy for several years and Ray and Lisa had decided they would get him a dog for Christmas.

Ray had never had a dog when he was growing up. His mother had raised him and his brother herself after their father had left them when he was eight years old. She worked two jobs and barely made enough money to support the three of them, never mind a dog. Besides, he had been afraid of dogs as a kid. His mother told him a dog had attacked him when he was two years old, though he didn't remember it, at least not consciously. He still had a faint scar on his arm to remind him, though.

Lisa had grown up with dogs and he knew she couldn't imagine a home without at least one dog in it. When they had met she had a mixed breed dog she had rescued from the pound. After he died, she had rescued Drake from the same pound. Two puppies would be a lot of work, but he couldn't say no to Jessica, it would break her heart.

Justin ran down the aisle of the pet store with Jessica only a few steps behind. There were colorful squeeze toys and chew toys of all shapes and sizes hanging on rows of hooks. It was like the candy aisle in the grocery store, with so many tempting objects to choose from. He had one thing in mind to buy for Marshmallow; a ball. The first trick he planned to teach him was how to fetch. He played fetch with Drake now and then, but as much as the older dog loved the game, his lame leg made it difficult.

While Jessica looked over the packaged chew toys, Justin moved down the aisle to the bins of different sized colored balls. He decided to get a medium sized rubber ball, one that Marshmallow could fit in his mouth, but would be too large for him to swallow. He hesitated at the bright red one—red used to be his favorite color. He selected a black one instead.

Justin walked back to where Jessica stood on tiptoe trying to grab a purple rubber ring. It was just out of her reach. He reached up and grabbed the ring for her.

"You should buy Fluffy a ball instead of this chew ring," Justin advised his sister, as he handed it to her. "I'm going to teach Marshmallow how to fetch. You could teach Fluffy how to fetch, too."

Jessica looked down at the rubber ring in her hand. "Do they have a purple ball?" she asked Justin.

"I'm sure they do," he replied. Jessica thought for a moment, and then handed the ring to her brother, who slipped it back on the hook. After a few minutes of searching through the bin, Justin found a purple ball. He handed it to his sister.

"It's perfect!" she exclaimed happily. "Thanks, Justin."

"No problem."

Next, Lisa took the kids to an aisle where there were rows of brightly colored collars and leashes—red, blue, purple, pink.

"Look at all the colors," Jessica exclaimed. "They look like hair ribbons." Justin picked out a black collar and leash for Marshmallow, and Jessica picked out purple ones for Fluffy.

Ray, who had gone to find a pet carrier, walked down the aisle toward his family. He held a gray carrier that had openings on the sides and top for ventilation and light.

"What do you think of this one?" he asked Lisa. "I thought it would be big enough to be comfortable, but small enough to fit in the back seat of the car with the kids. Besides, I wanted to find an inexpensive one since the dogs will outgrow it soon." Lisa looked the carrier over and tried the door latch.

"It seems fine to me," she said approvingly. "Let's go ring all of this stuff up before we go broke. I'll use the credit card so we don't have to dig into our travelers checks."

"Oh, no," Ray quickly insisted. "I brought some extra cash with me in case of an emergency."

"Okay," Lisa said with a shrug of her shoulders. She looked over at the checkout area. Only one register was open and there was a line of people waiting there. "Do you mind if the kids and I wait for you in the car?"

"Go ahead. I'll be out shortly. Hopefully," he said, eyeing the check-out line, which was growing longer by the minute.

CHAPTER 14

STEVE TOOK TOBY and Tara outside and put them in the pen while he cleaned the grill. After he was done, he opened the pen and let the puppies roam free in the yard while he watched them from the patio chair. The male was bigger and more energetic than his sister, but she didn't let him get more than a few feet away from her. Each time he ran off to explore, she would scamper after him.

After ten minutes or so, Steve decided his break was over. The crew would be arriving any minute. He pushed himself out of the chair and, after putting Toby and Tara back in the pen, went into the trailer.

The smell of boiled potatoes filled the air. Steve went into the kitchen where Sharon was putting the finishing touches on the potato salad.

"Looks good," he remarked, and reached over to pick up a chunk of potato from the bowl. "And tastes great!" he added with a grin.

"Hey! Knock it off!" Sharon chided, and gently slapped his hand. "There won't be any left after you're done picking."

He licked the remaining dressing from his fingers.

"Is the grill done?"

"Yes, ma'am. I'm here to report for further duty." Steve snapped his heels together and gave Sharon a crisp salute.

"You're incorrigible," Sharon said with a smile. "Are the dogs in the pen?"

"Yup. I let them run around the yard for a while." Steve looked out the kitchen window and saw both puppies curled up next to each other. "I guess all the activity tuckered them out. They're both sleeping now." Sharon came over to the window and stood next to Steve.

"I'm going to miss those guys. I've become attached to them already," she said.

"Me, too," Steve acknowledged. "It's amazing how fast they grow on you."

Just then, Max, the neighbor's dog, started barking. Steve looked out the window and saw the Grand Marquis pull into the driveway.

"They're here!" he exclaimed, and went out to greet their guests.

As soon as the car came to a stop, Justin and Jessica jumped out of the back seat and ran over to the pen.

"Come back and shut the doors!" their mother called after them. But they didn't hear her. By the time Lisa was out of the car, Justin had already returned.

"Hey, Dad, can you pop the trunk so I can get Marshmallow's ball?"

"I want Fluffy's ball, too," Jessica said, out of breath from trying to keep up with her brother.

Ray pushed the trunk release on the key fob.

"There you go," he said.

"You should go say hello to your aunt and uncle before you start playing with the puppies," their mother said, as Steve and Sharon came out of the trailer. Justin reached them first.

"Aunt Sharon, Uncle Steve, did you hear? Dad's letting us have the puppies, both of them!"

"Did we hear?" Steve replied. "It's the headline story of the day! Front page stuff!" Steve kidded Justin.

"Oh, Uncle Steve." Justin laughed.

"Don't pay any attention to him," Sharon said, and gave her nephew a big hug. Jessica ran up to where they stood on the trailer patio. She had Fluffy's purple ball in her hand.

"We can have the puppies!" she said excitedly.

"I know," replied Sharon. "Your mom called this morning to tell us the good news."

"I bought Marshmallow a ball at the pet store so I can teach him how to fetch," Justin announced.

"Me, too," Jessica said. "I picked out a purple ball for Fluffy. It matches the collar I bought her. I'm going to teach her to fetch, too."

"Okay. You kids go play with the puppies while your father and I help Uncle Steve and Aunt Sharon get ready for the cookout," Lisa said. Justin and Jessica gladly obeyed their mother and ran over to the puppies' pen. The adults headed into the trailer.

Justin opened the makeshift gate. Toby ran to him and jumped up on his shins, his tail wagging furiously. Justin bent over and picked up the excited puppy. Jessica went into the pen, swooped Tara into her arms and gave her a big squeeze. The puppy let out a small yelp.

"Be careful, Jess," Justin admonished her. "You're hurting Fluffy. She's not as big as Marshmallow."

"I'm sorry, Fluffy. I didn't mean to hurt you." She kissed Tara on the top of her head.

"Come on. Let's take them where there's more room." The two carried the puppies over to the side of the trailer that abutted the yard where Max lived. Justin placed Toby down in the grass and held the ball close to the dog's nose so he could smell it. Curious about the object, Toby inspected the ball. Having gained the puppy's attention, Justin gently tossed the ball several yards. Toby carefully watched the ball fly through the air and drop down to the ground. He ran to where it landed, sniffed at it, then picked the ball up with his mouth and ran back to Justin.

Justin jumped up and down. "He did it!" he exclaimed. "Marshmallow fetched the ball!" He bent down, gently took the ball from Toby's mouth, and threw it again. This time the ball went farther and landed by the edge of the trees behind the trailer. Again, Toby ran to the area where the ball landed and after a few moments of looking around, found it and ran back with it in his mouth.

"Good boy!" Justin praised Toby and picked him up with the ball still in his mouth. He kissed the puppy on the top of his head and set him back down.

"Let's see if Fluffy can fetch," Jessica said and put Tara down in the grass. She held the purple ball in front of Tara's nose the way her brother had done with Toby. Tara sniffed the ball cautiously for a moment, and then turned away.

"Fluffy, look." Jessica threw the ball with an underhand motion. It went up several yards in the air, but dropped only a couple of feet from where she stood. Toby, who had been watching the whole time, dropped his black ball on the ground and ran to get Tara's. Tara followed her brother.

"No, Marshmallow," Justin said, as he picked Toby up and took the ball from his mouth. "It's Fluffy's turn to fetch the ball." He handed the ball back to his sister. "This time throw the ball straight out like you did before, and I'll hold Marshmallow so he can't get it."

Jessica threw the ball again. This time it went straight out toward a copse of sycamore trees behind the trailer.

"Go get it, Fluffy," Jessica encouraged the puppy, but Tara just sat there looking up at her.

"Maybe if I let Marshmallow go for the ball again Fluffy will get the idea," Justin suggested.

"Okay," replied his sister.

Justin put Toby down.

"Go on, boy. Fetch the ball," Justin prodded, but Toby only looked up at him and stayed where he was.

"He probably didn't see where the ball went," Justin said. "Go get it and throw it again."

Jessica retrieved the ball and let each puppy sniff it before she stood up, cocked her arm behind her head, and threw the ball as hard as she could. But her arm crossed over her body, and the ball, instead of going straight, soared to the left into Max's yard and rolled to a stop by the neighbor's driveway.

Toby hesitated for a moment and then took off in a flash. Tara ran after him. She was several feet behind her brother when he reached the purple ball.

CHAPTER 15

THE BOY WAS BACK. Toby was excited to see him. The boy had a ball with him this time and started playing the same game the boy at the farm had played with him. Toby knew what to do. Each time the boy threw the ball, Toby would retrieve it so the boy could throw it again. This made the boy happy, which made Toby happy.

The girl had also brought a ball. The first time she threw it, Toby ran to the ball and brought it back. But instead of being happy, the boy seemed disappointed. Toby thought maybe he didn't retrieve the ball fast enough. He planned to run faster the next time. But the next time the girl threw the ball, the boy held Toby in his arms, preventing him from going after it. After a moment, the boy set Toby down next to Tara, and the girl went to get the ball. Now Toby was confused. Maybe we're supposed to take turns, he thought.

The girl threw the ball a third time. It soared into the next yard. Toby and Tara had not explored that area yet. It was where the barking had come from the past two nights. Toby hesitated for a moment, and then bolted after the ball, running as fast as he could. *I'm going to make the boy happy this time,* he thought.

Within a few seconds, Toby was upon the ball. The scent of the dog they had smelled earlier was strong here, but Toby was too intent on retrieving the ball to realize what that meant. As he bent his head to pick it up, he noticed another ball lying only a foot away. It was bigger than the one the girl had thrown. Toby was curious. He walked over to it, but just before he reached it, a low, rumbling sound came from his right.

Toby stopped and slowly turned his head in the direction of the sound. Several yards away, at the edge of the building, stood the biggest dog Toby had ever seen. He was all black, and his white teeth glared from between his snarling lips. Toby heard a small gasp behind him. Tara had followed him. He turned his head a little bit more and could see her out of the corner of his eye only a foot or so behind him. The growling became louder.

"Tara," Toby whispered. "When I yell 'go' run back to the boy and girl as fast as you can. Okay?"

"Okay." Her voice was barely audible.

"Are you ready?"

"Yes." Her voice was even quieter now.

"Go!" Toby yelled as loud as he could. He turned and fled. The dog began barking. Out of the corner of his eye, he saw the large animal bolt toward them. Tara had not moved. Toby turned back and watched in horror as the black dog pounced on her.

✧ ✧ ✧

JESSICA'S SCREAM brought Lisa up from the kitchen chair and through the trailer door in an instant.

"Jessica, what's wrong?" she called out to her daughter in a panic. Justin stood next to his sister with Toby in his arms. He yelled something to his mother and pointed toward the yard next door. A large, black dog was at the end of a taut chain. He had something on the ground under his paw. Something white.

"Oh, no!" Lisa cried out. "He's got Fluffy! Ray!"

Ray and Steve came running out of the trailer.

"Help me find something to threaten Max with," Steve said, his voice filled with urgency. "A stick or something."

"Here's a pole," Ray said, and tossed Steve a long metal rod he found leaning against the side of the trailer. It was a piece of post left over from the construction of the pen. Jessica, now in her mother's arms, cried out "Fluffy" over and over between heaving sobs.

Steve ran to where Max still held Tara down. He held the pole in front of the large, angry dog.

"Be careful, Steve!" Sharon called out from where she stood with Lisa and the kids. But Steve didn't hear her. He concentrated on approaching Max.

"Max!" he yelled, and waved the stick in front of the dog's face. "Let go of that puppy!" he commanded. Max just looked at him and growled. Steve pushed the stick against Max's mouth. The dog grabbed it with his teeth and whipped his head back and forth in an attempt to pull the stick from Steve's grasp. While he fought for the stick, Max momentarily forgot about his prey and removed his paws from Tara. Steve used the stick—still firmly clenched between the dog's teeth—to pull Max away from where Tara lay in the grass.

Ray, ignoring the trembling of his body and the fear that filled his mind, ran to where the small white puppy lay and grabbed her off the ground. The terror that had threatened to overcome him at the sight of the snarling black dog was suppressed by his daughter's pleas. Tears streamed down Jessica's face as he carried the puppy over to her.

"Is Fluffy . . . okay, Daddy?" she asked between sobs.

Ray placed Tara on the picnic table. The panic he had managed to stifle surfaced and his hands began to shake. "I'm not sure, honey. She seems to be okay." Ray gently examined Tara for any injuries as he tried to keep his hands from trembling. "I don't see any wounds."

"We'd better take her to a vet to be sure," said Sharon. "I'll go in and call the animal clinic up the street."

A white Cadillac pulled into the neighbor's driveway. Steve walked over to the huge car. He still had the pole tightly clenched in his hand. An older couple stepped out of the car, each with a puzzled expression.

Inside the trailer, Sharon dialed the number for the Southside Animal Hospital. A woman answered the phone.

"Southside Animal Hospital, can you hold, please?" The woman's voice was pleasant.

"Sure," Sharon replied automatically, then realized a moment too late she should have told her the call was an emergency. Light classical music began to play through the earpiece. Sharon peered out the kitchen window. Their neighbors, Mr. and Mrs. Wright, Max's owners, had come home. Steve was talking with them in their driveway. After a moment, Mr. Wright unhooked Max from the chain and walked him to the front of the trailer. His wife remained talking with Steve.

Sharon continued to watch out the window.

"May I help you?" The woman at the other end of the phone surprised Sharon out of her thoughts.

"Yes, my sister's puppy was just attacked by our neighbors' Doberman Pinscher. There's no blood or wounds as far as we can see, but we think she should be seen by a vet as soon as possible."

"Certainly. Bring her right over."

"Okay, we'll be there in a few minutes. Thank you."

After Steve explained to Mrs. Wright what had happened, they walked over to where Tara lay on the picnic table. Jessica gently stroked the top of the puppy's head. An errant tear occasionally fell down her face.

"Where's Sharon?" Steve asked.

"She's inside calling a vet," Ray replied.

"Is the puppy okay?" Mrs. Wright asked no one in particular, as she bent over the table.

"We're not sure," said Ray. "We don't see any injuries."

"Mrs. Wright, this is my brother-in-law, Ray, and his wife, Lisa, Sharon's sister, and their two children, Justin and Jessica. The puppy's name is Fluffy. She's Jessica's."

Mrs. Wright walked over to Jessica. "I'm so sorry this happened to your puppy," she said gently. "Max has never done anything like this before. I don't know what got into him."

"It was my fault," Jessica said. She sniffed and wiped a tear from her face. "I threw her ball into your yard by accident." Jessica looked down at her hands clasped in front of her.

"Don't blame yourself, child. You didn't do it intentionally. You probably didn't even know Max was outside, did you?" Mrs. Wright asked Jessica.

"No," she sniffed again.

"See? It was something that just happened. The unfortunate incident was nobody's fault, except maybe Max's. I don't understand why Max attacked poor Fluffy." Mrs. Wright paused for a moment, then shook her head and said, "Fluffy will be fine. You'll see." She patted the top of Jessica's head affectionately and turned to Steve.

"Mr. Wright and I will pay for the vet bill, of course."

"That's not necessary, Mrs. Wright. We . . ."

"I insist," she interrupted.

"Uncle Steve, can I go get Jessica's ball for her?" Justin asked. "It's still in Mrs. Wright's yard."

Steve looked at Mrs. Wright.

"Certainly, dear. Mr. Wright took Max in the house already. He's probably given him a good tongue-lashing by now."

Justin ran to where the purple ball still lay next to the driveway. He went to pick it up and saw a larger, brown ball nearby. The ball looked like it had been chewed by a bear. He picked up both balls and ran back to the picnic table.

"Look," he said, and held both balls out in front of him. "I found another ball near Fluffy's."

"Oh, that's Max's ball!" said Mrs. Wright in surprise. "That must be why Max went after poor Fluffy. He thought she was going to take his ball. Max just loves his ball. Well, that explains why he attacked her. I didn't think Max would be mean-spirited without a reason, not that it's a good one."

Sharon came out of the trailer.

"Hi, Mrs. Wright," she greeted her neighbor.

"Hi, dear. I'm so sorry about what happened. Did you find a vet to see her?"

"Yes, thank goodness. The Southside Animal Hospital said they can see her right away. They're only a few miles up the road."

"That's where we take Max. Dr. Vincent is wonderful with animals," she assured Sharon. "Well, I have to get back and see how Mr. Wright and Max are doing." She turned to Justin. "I'd better take Max's ball back to him. He likes to know where his beloved ball is at all times." Justin handed her the ball. She turned back to Sharon. "Let me know how the puppy makes out, will you?"

"Of course," Sharon replied. "We'll let you know as soon as we get back."

"Please do," Mrs. Wright said, and returned to her trailer.

"Steve, why don't Lisa and I take Fluffy to the vet while you and Ray watch the kids. I thought we'd take Marshmallow and also have him checked out. Okay?"

"Good idea," said Steve. Ray nodded in agreement. Jessica and Justin looked at each other.

"But we want to go to the vet with the puppies," said Justin.

"I think it's best if both of you stay here with your Uncle Steve and me," Ray replied. "Your mother and Aunt Sharon will be back with the puppies shortly. The important thing is to get Fluffy to the doctor."

A few minutes later, the Grand Marquis pulled out of the driveway with Lisa driving and Sharon sitting in the back seat next to the new pet carrier. As Jessica watched the car leave, a tear rolled down her face. She half-heartedly wiped it away with the back of her hand and went to look for consolation from her father.

CHAPTER 16

TOBY AND TARA LAY on a soft towel inside a container that had slats on all sides. They were inside the vehicle the boy and girl had arrived in. The unfamiliar smell of new plastic filled Toby's nostrils, but the only thing on his mind was Tara.

"Are you okay?" he asked his sister.

"My stomach hurts where that dog pressed his paw on me," she said.

Toby looked down in shame. He had watched in helpless horror while the huge black dog had pounced on his sister. And before he had been able to think what to do, the boy had grabbed him and taken him back to the other yard.

"I'm sorry I couldn't help you," he apologized to Tara. "The boy came and picked me up before I could do anything," he explained, trying to relieve the growing guilt he felt. It didn't work.

"What could you have done?" Tara asked. "You only would have been hurt yourself." She hesitated and inwardly winced in pain. She didn't want Toby to know how bad she

really felt. "What good would that have been?" she said.

"I don't know, but I should have done something."
Toby's voice was filled with regret.

"There's nothing you could have done," Tara insisted.

Toby knew his sister was right. The dog was too big.
Toby would have also been hurt, or worse, and Tara needed
him now, though he would have gladly traded places with
her.

"Where are we going?" Tara asked.

"As far away from that dog as possible, I hope," Toby
replied. He looked up through the slots in the top of the
carrier. The woman's face was partially visible. Toby liked
the woman. She was kind. He knew she wouldn't hurt them.
And the two men had rescued Tara. Toby had watched
while one had used a stick to lead the dog away from Tara,
and the other had grabbed her and taken her to safety.
Humans were good, he decided. It was other dogs they had
to watch out for.

The car went over a bump and came to a stop. Toby
looked up at the woman again and saw her hand come
down on top of the carrier. The carrier lurched upward.
Tara moaned, but before Toby could ask her if she was
okay, sunlight spilled through the openings and flashed in
his eyes. For a moment he couldn't see anything. Then as
quickly as the brightness had appeared, it vanished. Toby
blinked his eyes to adjust to the diminished light.

The muffled sound of a dog barking reached his ears.
He quickly looked at Tara. A wild look of fear was in her
eyes. Toby heard humans talking nearby. One of them was
the woman. Peering through one of the slats, Toby saw that
they were in some sort of building. A multitude of animal

smells wafted into the carrier. Dog, cat, and other animal scents mixed with the scent of humans.

"Where are we, Toby?" Tara asked. "What kind of place is this?"

"I don't know," Toby replied, as he peered out of the side of the carrier. But his only view was of a plain white wall a couple of feet away.

"Can you see anything on your side?" he asked Tara. But before she had a chance to look, the door of the carrier opened and a human hand reached in. The woman's sweet, soft voice flowed through the top of the carrier as the hand moved toward Tara. She shrank back. A man's face appeared in the opening. Tara cried out as the hand picked her up and slowly pulled her out. The door closed and Toby was alone.

✧ ✧ ✧

"IS THIS THE ONE that was attacked?" Dr. Vincent asked Sharon.

Sharon nodded her head in confirmation. "Yes. We're not sure if she's hurt or not. We didn't see any wounds when we checked her, but the dog had her down for several minutes."

"Was the dog big? About how much did it weigh?"

"Maybe 75 or 80 pounds. It was Mr. and Mrs. Wright's dog, Max. Mrs. Wright told me she takes him to you."

"Oh, yes, Max. He's a Doberman, right?"

"Yes, that's him."

"He's quite large compared to this little lady. Tell me exactly what happened." Dr. Vincent began to carefully examine the frightened puppy on the metal examination table. Sharon told him what she knew of the incident, as he gently picked up each of Tara's legs, one at a time. He felt along the length of them, slowly bending the joints. His fingers then gently probed her back, chest, and stomach area feeling for signs of injury.

"I don't see or feel any damage to her, but we'd better take some x-rays just in case. Sheila," he called to his assistant, "I need a couple of x-rays of this little lady."

"Be right there," his assistant called from the other side of the large examination room.

"We also brought her brother along," Sharon said to the doctor. "I was hoping you could give him a quick checkup, too. The puppies were both abandoned. We found them a few days ago on our way home from camping."

"Sure, I'll take a look at him," said Dr. Vincent. "Put him on the table here."

Sharon opened the carrier and took Toby out. She placed him on the table a short distance from his sister. Sheila walked over from the other side of the room to take Tara for her x-rays.

"Oh, aren't they beautiful!" she exclaimed. "What kind of dogs are they?" she asked Sharon.

"Well, actually, I was hoping you could tell us. We think they might be part German Shepherd, but we're not sure."

Dr. Vincent, who had begun examining Toby, said, "They're definitely part German Shepherd. It's hard to tell what the other part is. They could have some wolf-blood in them, but there's no way to know for sure."

"Wolf-blood?" Sharon asked in surprise.

"Wolf-blood?" Lisa echoed her sister.

"I'm sorry. I didn't mean to concern you. I worked in northern Minnesota for over ten years and there were a large number of wolf-hybrid dogs that people owned as pets in the area. There are breeders who actually specialize in breeding wolf-hybrids. Even in the wild, it's not uncommon for wolves to breed with domesticated dogs, especially German Shepherds. They look very similar, you know."

"What makes you think they're part wolf?" Sharon asked with concern.

"Well now, see what I've gone and done. I shouldn't have said anything. I'm not even sure if they are part wolf. Wolves and German Shepherds look very similar, but wolves have shorter, much bushier tails and the orbital angle of their skull is less than that of domesticated dogs. If these puppies do have any wolf blood in them, it's very little; probably none at all."

"Is that why they're white instead of black like most German Shepherds?" Sharon asked.

"No. White German Shepherds are more common than most people think. You said the dogs were abandoned. Where did you find them?"

"In northern California in a small town called Franklin."

"Well, there you go," Doctor Vincent said. "There aren't many wolves in northern California these days. I'm sure I'm wrong."

Sharon turned to Lisa. The look of concern on her sister's face remained. "But, if you're right, aren't wolves dangerous? Could the puppies grow up to be vicious?" Lisa asked the doctor.

Dr. Vincent stopped examining Toby for a moment. "First of all, wolves aren't a real danger to humans. Attacks on humans are rare and have occurred only in extreme circumstances where their natural food supply is scarce or non-existent. The bad reputation wolves have comes from the fact that they kill domesticated animals—sheep and such—since domesticated animals are typically more vulnerable than wild prey." He paused a moment to prevent Toby from falling off the edge of the table where he had wandered during his reprieve from the doctor's scrutiny. "I wouldn't worry if I were you."

Lisa looked at Sharon.

"What are you going to do?" Sharon asked.

Lisa looked down at the puppies on the examination table. They were so cute and innocent. She couldn't imagine either of them hurting a thing. Her finger went to her lips as she thought a moment, and then said, "The kids would be devastated if we told them they couldn't keep the puppies. I guess I'll have to trust your opinion, Dr. Vincent."

When Dr. Vincent finished his examination of Toby he said, "This little guy is as healthy as they come. He's going to need to have some shots, of course. So will his sister. But I think you should wait a few weeks until she's over the trauma from her attack. Can you bring them back then?"

"Actually, we're just out here visiting. We plan on leaving tomorrow to go back to Connecticut. I'll have to take them to a vet back home. Will Fluffy be able to travel?"

"Are you traveling by plane?" the doctor asked.

"No, we drove out here. But we bought a pet carrier to keep the dogs in during the trip back."

Dr. Vincent rubbed his chin with his forefinger and thumb. "As long as I don't see any problems on the x-rays, car travel should be okay, though x-rays don't always pick up everything. Sometimes you just have to go by how the animal behaves and whether they seem to be in pain. Keep her as calm and quiet as possible, and if there's any sign of bleeding in the rectal area, or if she doesn't start to perk up significantly in a few days, you'd better take her to another vet."

Sheila walked out of the x-ray room with Tara cradled in her arms. She placed her next to Toby on the table.

"When will you know the results of the x-rays?" Lisa asked.

"I'll be able to review them after my next appointment, so leave a number where I can reach you with the receptionist. And as I said, don't worry about what I said about the possibility of these puppies being part wolf. They're both going to make great pets."

Ray sat in the lounge chair with his daughter on his lap.

"Is Fluffy going to be all right, Daddy?" she asked him.

"Sure, honey. She'll be fine," Ray assured her, but he wasn't as confident as he sounded. For Jessica's sake he hoped the puppy would be okay. His daughter would be devastated if the puppy died, and Ray couldn't stand to see her hurt. He would do anything for his daughter. Even give up drinking as it had turned out.

His father had been an alcoholic, as had his father's father. The branches of the Johnson family tree hung low with men and women whose lives had been devastated by alcohol and the violence it wrought on their families. Ray's paternal uncle had spent the remainder of his life in jail after shooting and killing a neighbor over a boundary dispute. Ray's own life had come perilously close to the precipice of no return. The blackouts had increased in number and length of time as he got older. Full days of his life were gone to him—time he would never get back—and his memories of the kids as babies were blurry at best. That was his biggest regret. And the compulsive gambling that accompanied many of his binges had caused additional financial problems for the family. But when he had finally reached the edge of the black yawning hole that called to him, he had turned away because of his daughter.

The incident had occurred several years earlier after he and Lisa had one of many arguments about how much money he spent on alcohol. At the height of the fight, Ray stalked out and went to his favorite bar, Charlie's Place. It was a small place. Not quite a hole in the wall, but close. Mostly locals hung out there. Every once in a while a strange face or two would come in for a couple of drinks, but that was it.

Ray knew everyone there. No one gave him a hard time about his drinking or gambling, although Joe, the bartender, occasionally shut Ray off when he believed he had too much to drink. The night of the big fight had been one of those times. Not only had Joe refused to serve Ray any more drinks, he had kicked him out of the bar and told him to go home. And Ray did. Things would have turned out better if he had just slept off the drunken stupor in an alley somewhere.

Lisa had still been up when he stumbled through the back door that night. As soon as he entered the living room where she sat waiting for him, they started fighting about his drinking and the money and how his behavior was ruining their marriage and their family life. The end result had been a floor lamp going through the living room picture window and Lisa screaming, which woke the kids and brought them downstairs.

The look of horror on Jessica's face when she saw the broken window and her mother crying partially sobered him. He went to her and hugged her tightly, promising her over and over he would never do anything like that again. There had been times since then when the urge to drink had tempted him, he couldn't deny it; especially recently since business had slowed and he had lost a couple of clients because of the lagging economy. Money was definitely tight and, after losing at the casino their last day in Vegas, would be even tighter after he got the credit card bill. But as long as he could hold onto his largest account, Schaeffer Electronics, things would be okay. And whenever he felt the tug of his alcoholism pull at him, he remembered his pledge to his daughter.

Now, Ray looked down at Jessica sitting in his lap and kissed the top of her head. He hugged her close to him.

"They're back! They're back!" Justin yelled, as he ran down the driveway, returning from his vigilant watch for the Grand Marquis. Jessica jumped off her father's lap and sprinted to where her brother stood waiting.

"Is Fluffy okay, Mommy?" Jessica anxiously asked her mother through the open car window.

"Let's put them into the trailer first, and then we'll tell

you everything the doctor said, okay?"

"Okay," she said reluctantly.

Once inside the trailer, Sharon carefully took Tara out of the pet carrier and placed her in the box. Toby ran out of the carrier on his own accord, and Justin picked him up and gave him a big hug. Jessica sat next to the box and gently stroked the top of Tara's head as Lisa described their visit to the animal hospital and all that the doctor had said, except for his comments about the possibility of the puppies having wolf-blood in them.

"Dr. Vincent said he'd call shortly with the results of the x-rays," Sharon said, as she stood up from sitting on the floor next to Jessica. "I don't know about the rest of you, but I'm starving. I didn't make all of that potato salad for nothing, did I? Why don't we start the cookout while we wait?"

"Good idea," Steve said, as he rose from the couch. "I'll fire up the grill so we can start cooking the hamburgers and hot dogs. Do you want to help me, Ray?"

"Sure," Ray replied, rising from the couch where he had been sitting next to Steve. "I make a pretty mean cheeseburger."

"Lisa and I will take care of everything else," said Sharon.

Sharon headed into the kitchen. As she walked past the telephone, it rang. Everyone froze. Sharon picked up the handset.

"Hello?"

There was a short pause.

"This is Mrs. Patterson."

There was another, longer pause.

"I see," said Sharon.

Sharon stood in the small hallway with her back to the alert group behind her. Everyone's attention was riveted on her.

Finally, she said, "Okay, thanks for all of your help. Good-bye." She turned toward the living room. Everyone looked at her in anticipation.

"She's okay!"

"Fluffy's okay!" Jessica jumped up and down. Justin's smile stretched from one side of his face to the other. There was a collective sigh of relief in the room as Sharon continued. "The doctor didn't see anything wrong on the x-rays, but she needs to rest and take it easy for a few days."

"Oh, thank goodness," Lisa said, and let out a deep breath.

Jessica went over to where Tara rested in the box and bent down to pick her up.

"Jessica, I think you should leave Fluffy alone for a while," her mother advised.

"Yes, Jessica," Sharon enjoined, "the doctor said she should stay quiet and calm."

"All right," Jessica said. "I'm just so excited that she's okay."

"I know," Sharon said. "Why don't you sit next to the box with her? I'm sure she'd like that."

"Okay." Jessica sat down next to the box.

Steve jumped up from the couch. "Well, now we have a real reason to celebrate. Let the cookout begin!"

Sharon picked up the telephone and began dialing. "I'd better call Mrs. Wright and let her know Fluffy's okay. I'm sure she's anxious to hear."

"Don't bother," said Steve. "I'll run over and tell them in person after I start the grill."

Sharon hugged Lisa tightly. After a moment she released her sister and placed her hands on her shoulders. "Make sure you call me as soon as you get home to let me know you arrived safely and how Fluffy's doing."

"I will," Lisa promised.

Steve and Ray stood nearby. Steve shook his brother-in-law's hand. "I hope you have a good trip back. It looks like a great day for traveling."

Ray looked up and scanned the morning sky. "It sure does," he replied. There wasn't a cloud in sight. The day promised to be perfect.

Justin and Jessica came running from the car where they each had been busy arranging their space in the back seat for the trip back home. When Jessica reached her Aunt Sharon, she raised her arms up to her. Sharon leaned down, picked up her niece and swung her around. Jessica's blonde hair flew straight out around her head and she let out a small shriek. After one spin, Sharon set Jessica down.

"I have a feeling the next time I see you I won't be able to do that. You're getting too big, and I'm getting too old," Sharon complained, rubbing her lower back.

"You're not too old, Aunt Sharon," Jessica objected. "You'll never be too old."

Sharon laughed and gave her one last hug. "You're a sweetheart!"

Justin came over to say good-bye to his aunt. Sharon

gave him a hug and kiss. "Hopefully we won't have to wait too long before we see you two again. You're both growing up so quickly," she said.

Steve, having just finished giving Jessica a hug and kiss, came over to Justin and put out his hand. Justin shook it, and Steve clasped his nephew with his left arm and hugged him. "You take care of yourself, sport. And take care of that puppy of yours. I want you to send us pictures of Marshmallow and Fluffy as they grow, okay?"

"Sure, Uncle Steve," Justin replied. "I can take the pictures with the new camera I got for my birthday."

After everyone said their good-byes, the group moved to the car. The pet carrier, with Toby and Tara securely settled inside, sat directly in the middle of the back seat separating Justin and Jessica's space. Steve and Sharon had said good-bye to the puppies earlier.

"Are you sure you have everything?" Sharon asked her sister one last time. "I gave you the small bowls for the dogs' food and water, right?"

"Yup," Lisa replied. "I think we're all set!"

Ray got into the car and started the engine. The kids climbed into the back seat. Sharon gave Lisa one last hug. Tears welled up in Sharon's eyes. She wished her sister lived closer. She was going to miss her. Steve put his arm around Sharon as the car backed out of the driveway.

"Bye!" the kids yelled out the back window, waving their arms wildly.

"Good-bye!" Steve and Sharon called out in unison, as the car drove down the trailer park road. They waved until the car was out of sight.

PART IV
Innocence Lost

✧ ✧ ✧

"There is an Indian legend which says when a human dies
there is a bridge they must cross to enter into heaven.
At the head of that bridge waits every animal
that human encountered during their lifetime.
The animals, based upon what they know of this person,
decide which humans may cross the bridge...
and which are turned away..."

— *Unknown*

CHAPTER 17

THE PAIN WAS WORSE now, almost unbearable. Tara knew something bad had happened inside her when the dog pinned her down, and the injury left her weak and exhausted. She tried to keep her suffering to herself, but Toby knew something was terribly wrong with his sister. He asked her over and over how she felt, and each time she replied that she felt fine. But Toby heard the soft, whimpering sounds she made while she slept and saw her wince whenever the car went over a bump, even a small one.

Two days had passed since their new journey began. As the third day wore on, Tara's condition deteriorated. Toby instinctively knew his sister, the only family member he had left, was dying, and there was nothing he could do to change that fact. If only he could have saved her from the attack; if only the boy hadn't picked him up when he wanted to go help his sister, maybe he'd be the one dying instead of her. He would never be able to forgive himself for not saving her. Toby closed his eyes and dropped his head between his front paws as he mourned for his sister and for himself. Blanketed in sorrow, he fell asleep.

Tara lay in the corner opposite her brother. She hadn't changed her position since the start of the trip that morning. Movement hurt. Most of the time she slept, unless the pain awakened her, as it had a moment ago when the carrier was jarred again by a bump in the road. She watched Toby sleep. She knew he blamed himself for the attack, but there was nothing he could have done.

Her eyelids grew heavy again, and as she began to drift back to sleep, a soft, warm glow slowly descended upon her. The light encompassed her, cradled her in its warmth, and lifted her up and out of the pain-racked body that encumbered her. She felt as if she were floating. The fear she would normally expect to feel was absent, and thankfully, so was the pain. She remained in this blissful state for an indeterminate period, and then found herself back on the farm. Back with her mother and brothers and sisters, reliving the moments she had treasured most in her short life. As the memories continued, another lifetime passed by. She wanted to stay there forever, but knew she couldn't remain, for this was her past; her future lay ahead. Tara reluctantly let go of the happy memories and slowly drifted back to the present and to Toby. She knew she didn't have much time left with him. Quietly, she called out to her brother, "Toby . . . are you awake?"

Toby lifted his head and became instantly alert. "Are you okay?" he asked, panic laced his voice.

"I'm fine, Toby . . . I was just dreaming . . . about the farm and Mama. You and I were both back there and . . . and everything was wonderful again." Tara's voice was *weak, and she spoke between short, shallow breaths. "The dream seemed so real."*

Toby looked at his sister, his eyes filled with love and tears.

Tara tried to gather up enough energy to speak again. "I just ... wanted ... to tell you," she began. Then abruptly, she sat up.

"Did you hear that?" she asked Toby.

"Hear what?"

"Somebody called my name."

"I didn't hear anything."

"There it is again. The voice is louder now." Tara stared straight ahead, her eyes focused, as if she could see through the walls of the carrier. "I see them Toby. They're coming for me." Head cocked, Toby looked at the side of the box where his sister's gaze was affixed. He saw nothing.

"Who's coming? I don't see anyone."

Tara continued to watch as the vision came in focus. One by one, figures of wolves and dogs of various shapes and sizes appeared before her within a large glowing sphere of light. As the group came together, two individuals stood out among the rest, a male and a female. The male was large and white and had a gentle fierceness about him. The female was black and smaller and stood proudly next to her mate. They beckoned Tara to join them. She started forward, unafraid. As she approached the figures, the same soft, warm glow she had experienced earlier enveloped her and filled her with a powerful feeling of love. She turned back and saw Toby looking at the body she had left behind, his head still endearingly tilted to the side. She wanted to describe to her brother how serenely beautiful this new world was and beckon him to come with her, but Tara knew this was her time, not his. One day he would walk the same path and they would be together again, forever.

Toby sensed the transformation occurring in Tara. A look of serenity lay upon her face. He thought she looked at him one last time before the light in her eyes went out and her body gently sagged down, her head coming to rest on her paws. She was gone. For a few grateful moments, Toby only felt numbness, but it was quickly replaced by a tidal wave of grief that engulfed him. An uncontrollable wail rose from the depth of his being.

JESSICA WAS RESTLESS. She had colored some of the pictures in her coloring book and played with her stuffed animals to occupy herself, but now she was bored. An hour earlier, her mother had announced they were entering New Mexico and, as usual, proceeded to read from one of the numerous tour books she had brought along on the trip. As Jessica stared out the window, she tried to pay attention to what her mother was saying, but only half heard what she said. Her thoughts were elsewhere.

Justin sat next to her with his earphones on, listening to music and reading a comic book. He was no fun. A couple of years ago he would have been willing to play car games with her, but not now. He said he was too old for those silly games. Jessica bent over the pet carrier and peered through one of the holes on top. Why is Fluffy still sleeping? she wondered. She's been sleeping all day. "Fluffy," she called quietly. "Wake up." But the puppy didn't stir.

Jessica sat up in her seat and took another sip from her juice box. She stared out the car window and watched the scenery flash by. She couldn't wait to get home and show her new puppy to her friends, especially her best friend, Amelia. Amelia had a dog, too. A big one, like the one that had attacked Fluffy, but Amelia's dog was friendly and always licked Jessica when she visited.

"Hey, Jessica," Justin said, startling his sister out of her thoughts. He had taken off his earphones and was looking into the pet carrier. "Have you noticed Fluffy hasn't moved all morning? Do you think she's okay?"

"She's just extra tired from that dog attacking her. Mom said it was a 'traumatic' experience. That means it was very bad."

"But she hasn't moved in a long time."

"She's okay," Jessica insisted.

"Still, we'd better have Ma take a look at her the next time we stop just to make sure."

In the front seat, Lisa, who had taken over the driving at the last rest stop, softly sang along to a country-western station she had found on the radio. Ray was stretched out across the rest of the front seat, asleep. His snoring had just started to grow in volume and strength, when a loud howl filled the car. Ray jerked up. "What was that?"

Lisa turned off the radio. "What's going on back there? Is everything all right? Are the puppies okay?"

"Marshmallow must have made the noise. Fluffy's still sleeping in the corner. She hasn't moved all morning."

Lisa quickly glanced into the back seat. "I'd better pull over to make sure she's okay," she said.

Lisa pulled the car off onto the side of the deserted roadway. She jumped out of the car, took the carrier out, and placed it on the ground several yards away from the road. She crouched down and opened the small door. Toby was closest to her. Behind him, Tara lay still and quiet in the back corner. Lisa stiffened. Her heart dropped. A horrible sense of foreboding filled her.

She reached into the carrier, picked up Toby, and handed him to Justin, who now stood next to her. "Hold him," she said, "and don't set him down." She reached into the back of the carrier and softly placed her hand on Tara's body. The puppy did not stir. Lisa's apprehension grew. She slipped her hand under Tara's stomach and slowly lifted her up. The lifeless body hung limp in her hand. Lisa turned and looked at her daughter standing on the other side of her. Jessica knew by the look on her mother's face that something was terribly wrong.

"What's wrong, Mommy?" she asked, as she dropped to the ground on her hands and knees. She peered past her mother into the pet carrier and caught a glimpse of the puppy's body hanging from her mother's hand.

Lisa didn't know what to say. Still holding Tara, she pulled her hand out of the carrier. "Jessica," she started. "Fluffy . . . is . . ." She stopped and looked up at her daughter.

"She's dead, isn't she?" Jessica cried out.

"I'm so sorry, honey. She must have been more hurt than the doctor thought."

Jessica turned to her father standing behind her and flung her arms around his waist. With her head against his stomach, she sobbed uncontrollably. Ray put one arm around her shoulder and stroked her hair with the other hand. After several minutes, Jessica pulled herself from his hold and turned back to her mother who now held the small, lifeless pup in the crook of her arm. Jessica's face was red and swollen, her blue eyes rimmed in red. Tears rolled down her cheeks and dropped onto the front of her T-shirt forming dark, wet splotches. She quickly wiped the tears from one side of her face and held out her arms to her mother.

"Let me see her. I want to hold her." Jessica's small body heaved with a heavy sob as she bravely waited to hold her lost puppy. Lisa reached out and gently placed Tara's body in her daughter's outstretched arms. Jessica cradled it while she cried, "Poor Fluffy. Poor, poor . . . Fluffy."

Justin went over to his sister. He groped for the right words to say, words that would somehow make her feel better. He tried to imagine how he would feel if Marshmallow had died, but the thought of that happening was too horrible.

"I'm sorry, Jess," he said quietly. "I know how you must feel."

Jessica looked up at her brother standing next to her with Toby in his arms, alive and healthy. She looked down at Tara, limp and dead. Anger welled up within her.

"You don't know how I feel!" she yelled at him. "Your puppy's not dead like mine!"

"Your brother's only trying to help you feel better, honey," Lisa said gently.

"Nothing will make me feel better!" she lashed out. "Nothing!" Jessica turned away from her family, then turned back to face them. "The only thing that would make me feel better is if Fluffy came alive again."

Lisa knelt in front of Jessica and held her daughter by the shoulders. "You know that can't happen, sweetheart. Once something dies, it can't come back to life."

"But where is she?" Jessica sniffed and looked into her mother's eyes. "Where did she go?" She searched for an answer to the pain she felt.

"No one knows for sure where things go when they die, but if she was hurt and in a lot of pain, I'm sure she's happier now wherever she is." Lisa stroked the dead puppy's fur.

"Will I get to see her when I die? Will I go to the same place she goes?"

Lisa selected her words carefully. "I believe all living things come from the same place and return to the same place. So eventually, all things come together again when they die."

"So I will see Fluffy again?" Jessica asked, hope restored in her voice.

"I believe you will, Jessica," Lisa said. "I believe you will."

Jessica kissed Tara on the head and handed her back to her mother.

"We have to bury her, Jess," Lisa said slowly, wondering how her daughter would react.

"Can we bury her at home in the back yard?"

"No, sweetie, we can't wait that long. She needs to be buried right away." Lisa looked up at Ray.

"Your Mom's right, honey," Ray said. "We won't be home for three more days. We can't wait that long. We have to bury her now." He scanned the area for a suitable spot.

"We can bury her over there in the clearing among those shrubs," he said, pointing to a group of short stubby trees amidst scattered tufts of dried scrub grass. He didn't know what he'd dig the grave with. Hopefully the car at least had a tire iron.

He turned to Lisa. "I'll go look for something in the trunk to dig with." Then he lowered his voice. "See if you can find a small box or bag to put the body in so we can bury her properly for Jessica."

"Okay," she replied.

Ray opened the trunk. The well was jam packed with their luggage and sundry travel gear.

"Justin," Ray called for his son. "Would you please help me take this stuff out of the trunk so I can find something to dig with?"

"Sure, Dad."

Justin reluctantly placed Toby back in the pet carrier and closed the door. "I'll be back in a minute, boy," he promised, and went to help his father.

Lisa and Jessica looked in the car for a suitable container in which to bury the puppy, who lay on a small towel in the sand.

"Mommy," Jessica called, "can we bury Fluffy in my drawing box?"

Lisa looked over at her daughter who held the old shoe box she kept her drawing materials in: crayons, pencils, erasers, and a small ruler.

"Sure, that's a great idea. We'll just need to find something to put your stuff in." Lisa looked around and found an empty plastic bag. "Here, put your drawing stuff in this bag. The bag isn't as good as the box, but . . ."

"That's okay," Jessica interrupted. "I want Fluffy to have my drawing box. It's just the right size for her."

"Here we go," Ray announced, as he stood up from the trunk and held out a small metal spade probably meant for shoveling snow.

Once the hole was dug, Jessica kissed the top of Tara's head and gently placed her in the shoe box. She handed the box to her father, who placed the container in the hole.

The hardest part for Ray was listening to Jessica cry as he shoveled the dirt back into the hole. Seeing his daughter upset pained him more than anything. But Lisa consoled her while he finished the job, and in less than an hour, they were back on the road again.

✧　✧　✧

TOBY HAD NEVER felt so sad and alone before. Not when his brothers and sisters had been sold. Not even when he had been taken from his mother and their home. Tara had been there with him through all those losses and her presence had helped him deal with his grief. He had stayed strong for her; she had needed him to. And now, she was gone, as was his strength. All that was left of his family was gone. Everything that was important to him was gone. Toby couldn't imagine ever being happy again. Buried beneath the immense weight of grief, he was no longer the joyous, carefree puppy he had been just two days earlier.

Toby turned his head and looked through the pet carrier opening. The car carried him forward again. Where to, he didn't know. What to, he didn't care. Life had lost its meaning for him.

CHAPTER 18

THE REMAINDER OF the trip passed uneventfully and on the sixth day of their journey they were only a few miles from the Connecticut border. Jessica had been quiet the first couple of days after the death of her puppy, but she began to perk up after Justin told her he would share Marshmallow with her, and now she seemed almost back to her old self. She held Toby on her lap as the family eagerly awaited to cross the state line into Connecticut.

"There's the sign," Lisa announced. "Welcome to Connecticut!"

"We're home!" Justin and Jessica cried out from the back seat as the sign whizzed past.

"How long before we get there?" asked Justin.

"About an hour," his father responded.

"Are we going to pick up Drake before we go home?" Justin couldn't wait to see Drake and introduce the new puppy to him. He hoped they liked each other.

"We don't have time," Lisa answered. "The kennel closes at six and it's five o'clock now. Besides, there's no room for him in the car with all this stuff. We'll pick him up first thing tomorrow morning. You can come with me to get him up if you want."

"Okay. I can't wait for him to meet Marshmallow. I hope Drake likes him," said Justin. "He's probably wondering where we are since we've been gone so long. I hope he doesn't think we deserted him."

An hour later, Ray pulled the car into their driveway.

✧   ✧   ✧

THE MOVEMENT of the carrier woke Toby as it was lifted up and out of the car. He raised his heavy head for a moment, and then laid it back down. He had no interest in what was happening around him. All he wanted was to go back to his dreams about the farm where his pain was forgotten. There, he found his only solace. But his attempt to go back to sleep was thwarted by the opening of the carrier door. A hand grabbed him and pulled him out. It belonged to the boy, who bestowed hugs and kisses upon him. Before, Toby would have welcomed them. Now, the affectionate gestures could not reach through his emotional numbness.

A few minutes later, Toby found himself in a room surrounded by two large, very curious looking creatures. The two cats, Meesha and Pinka, slowly circled Toby, examining him from several feet away.

"What is it?" Pinka asked her sister.

"It's a dog," Meesha responded.

"I've never seen a white dog before," said Pinka.

"Well, it's a dog nonetheless. Look at the nose and ears

and tail. What else can it be?"

"Do you think it's going to live here?" asked Pinka.

"I don't know," replied Meesha.

The two discussed Toby as if he wasn't there. Their behavior irritated him. He couldn't take much more.

"Stop walking around me!" Toby lashed out at them and snapped his jaw in their direction. The two cats jumped back in surprise.

"There's no need to get huffy," said Meesha. "After all, this is our house." She lifted her nose up several degrees and looked down at Toby with her bright blue eyes. "We're only trying to figure out what you are."

"Why don't you just ask me then?"

"Okay, what are you?"

"My name is Toby, and yes, I am a dog. A white dog," he stressed, holding his head high and proud.

"See, I told you he's a dog," Meesha boasted to Pinka.

Pinka continued to examine Toby. "Why are you white?" she asked him.

"Don't be so insensitive, Pinka. Obviously he's very sick since there's no such thing as white dogs. Well, at least I've never seen one."

"I'm not sick!" Toby retorted. "And there are such things as white dogs; my sister Tara was white, too."

"Where is this sister of yours?" asked Meesha. "Why isn't she with you?"

Toby dropped his head. He didn't want to talk about Tara with these two cats. He didn't want to talk about her with anyone. "She didn't come with me. She's back on the farm," Toby replied. He hoped the two cats would now leave him alone. No such luck.

"Well, I don't know if I believe you or not. But it doesn't really matter why you're all white, does it? The fact is, you are, and the condition is quite unusual, so you can't expect others not to talk about it. Better to have others talk about you in front of your back than behind it I always say."

"I've never heard you say that before, Meesha," her sister remarked.

"That's because you don't listen. I say it all the time."

Toby was tired of listening to them. "Well, I think you two look quite unusual also," he retorted. "I've never seen cats with blue eyes before." Of course, the only cats he had ever seen were Cookie and her kittens, and their eyes were golden.

"All purebred Siamese cats have blue eyes," said Meesha.

Toby had no interest in what the cats had to say and unsuccessfully tried to ignore them.

"How did you get all white? Were your parents white?" Pinka asked.

"If I answer your question, will you leave me alone?" Toby asked.

"If that's what you want. But I think you should be civil to us if we're all going to be living here together," Meesha said. "Go on then, answer the question."

"My mother was black. I never met my father. He wasn't from the farm I lived on. But my mother told me that my grandfather was a white wolf named Strider," Toby said.

"A wolf? Oh, my!" Meesha turned to her sister. "Do you think he could be dangerous?"

But Pinka didn't have a chance to reply.

"There you go again! Talking as if I'm not here!" Toby said angrily.

"Oh, dear! We're making him angry. If he's dangerous, we certainly don't want to make him angry," said Meesha.

"I'm not dangerous. If I were, I would have eaten the two of you by now after all the aggravation you've given me!" Toby snapped at them.

For a moment, there was nothing but silence.

Meesha spoke first, addressing her sister. "He's right, you know. We'd better be nice to him if he's going to be living here." She turned to Toby. "My name is Meesha, and this is my sister, Pinka. We're the resident cats. Drake isn't here right now, but you'll meet him soon, I'm sure."

"What makes you think I'm going to be living here?" Toby asked.

"Why else would you be here?"

"I don't know. I've been taken so many different places recently, I figured I'd be taken somewhere else again soon," Toby replied, then asked, "Who's Drake?"

"He lives here, too," said Meesha. "A word of warning though, the spot under that table over there," she lifted her paw toward a table in the corner of the room, "is Drake's sleeping spot. I'd stay away from there if I were you." Meesha motioned to Pinka and the two cats turned and leisurely walked out of the room.

Toby didn't know what to make of his new situation. Another new home? For the first time since Tara's death, he was distracted from the unrelenting depression and grief he had been mired in. He was curious about this Drake the cats kept referring to. Was he another cat? Toby hoped not; two cats were more than enough. Maybe he was a dog, *like himself. Toby had detected another dog's scent when he entered the house. He walked around the room, sniffing the carpet and furniture as he went. The scent of the dog was strong in the carpet, and it became stronger as he approached the corner of the room where the table stood. Toby stopped. The spot under the table seemed forbidden to him. But his curiosity won over, and he cautiously moved closer. He was so focused on the strong dog smell coming from the corner, that he didn't hear the footsteps of the boy behind him. Suddenly, he was in the boy's arms and being carried up the stairs to the boy's bedroom.*

Drake liked to stay at the kennel, even though at times it was quite noisy. The younger dogs liked to show off their prowess by having contests to see who could bark the loudest, or longest, or fiercest. The games were all in good fun, but Drake and some of the other older dogs didn't have the energy or desire to participate in them anymore. Anyway, they seemed kind of silly; grown dogs making all that noise. A dog couldn't get a decent rest with all that barking going on. As the barking became louder, Drake decided to go back into his pen. He stood up and stretched his stiff front legs, then tried to give his rear legs a slight stretch, but the movement was difficult for him. His back left leg, which had been broken as a puppy, hindered him. The break had never healed properly, and the lame leg prevented Drake from running and playing like normal dogs. But he didn't miss running anymore; memories of running before the accident were dim and faraway, from another life. Besides, he had learned to accommodate his handicap over the years and had overcome many of the restrictions the lame leg placed upon him.

Drake entered through the opening in the exterior wall that led to his pen and lay down in the corner to rest. He wondered when his family would come and get him. Over three weeks had passed since they dropped him off at the kennel. He had never been left away from them that long before. Usually, they were only gone a few days, a week at the most.

Drake envied Meesha and Pinka. They were allowed to stay home when the family went away. The nice woman who lived next door went over every day to feed them and give them fresh water, and the small flap in the back door allowed the cats to go in and out of the house as they pleased. Drake had tried to fit through the opening once, but the hole was too small for his body, and he had almost become stuck.

The latch of Drake's pen clicked open. One of the kennel aides opened the door. She had Drake's leash in her hand. He was going home! The aide hooked the leash onto Drake's collar and led him to the front room where his family always met him. There they were: the woman, the boy, and the little girl. His family.

Drake pulled on his leash. His tail wagged furiously, and he panted heavily from the excitement. The boy ran up to Drake and hugged him around the neck. Drake licked him several times on the side of his face. The little girl and the woman also took turns hugging him. A few minutes later they were all outside. Drake recognized the family car parked a short distance from the kennel door. When they reached the vehicle, the boy opened the back door and Drake climbed in. One thing his lame leg hadn't prevented him from doing was going for rides in the car.

An unfamiliar scent filled the car; the scent of another dog. A plastic carrier sat on the back seat next to the other door. Drake could see a small white animal through the openings in the side. He moved over next to the cage as the boy climbed into the back seat with him. Once settled in, Drake looked down through the slats in the top of the cage and saw the face of a small, white dog gazing up at him. The dog appeared quite young.

"Who are you?" Drake whispered to the puppy.

The car engine started up

"My name's Toby," Toby whispered once the car started moving. He recognized Drake's scent to be the one he had smelled in the house. He was a big dog, much larger than Toby. Most of his fur was black with several white spots on his chest and head.

"Are you Drake?" he asked the dog.

"Yes. My mother named me Prince, but the family has been calling me Drake for so long . . . How do you know my name?"

"The two cats told me about you," Toby replied. "Well, they didn't actually tell me much about you other than your name, but they spoke as if you were very mysterious and quite dangerous."

"Those two are always exaggerating. You can't believe half of what they say. They love to gossip and make up stories." Drake paused and considered Toby for a minute. "Are you going to be living with us?"

"I don't know. That's what Meesha and Pinka said."

Their conversation was interrupted when the car stopped, and the boy jumped out of the car.

✧　✧　✧

THAT'S A GOOD sign, Justin thought after Drake climbed into the car and began to sniff the pet carrier. Since Justin had expected Drake to be upset and start growling when he first noticed the puppy, he was encouraged by Drake's reaction. He wanted the two dogs to become friends. Justin watched Drake continue to sniff through the top of the carrier as the car turned down their road.

As soon as they were all out of the car, Justin took the dogs into the back yard where his father had fenced in a large area for Drake. Drake's tail wagged as Justin opened the gate.

"You're hoping it's play time, aren't you, old boy?" Justin asked, as he patted the top of Drake's head. Justin smiled as he pushed the gate open and let the old dog go before him. With Toby in his arms, he turned and shut the gate. Drake went over and stood in the shade near the old wooden swing that hung from one of the long knobby limbs of an old oak tree. There had been many days in summers past when Justin had sat in that swing while furiously pumping his legs back and forth in an attempt to touch one of the large overhanging branches with the toe of his sneaker. His father had raised the swing higher each year as Justin grew. It was overdue for an adjustment.

Justin set Toby down next to Drake and walked over to the swing. He knew he couldn't force the dogs to get along. Any friendship that developed would have to happen naturally. He sat down on the swing sideways and pushed against the ground with his right foot causing the swing to go back. At the apex of the push, he lifted his foot and swung forward. He watched the two dogs sniff each other as he swung back and forth.

As the swing's momentum slowed, he saw the puppy raise his paw up to the older dog in a sign of playfulness. At first, Drake didn't respond. But then, after a moment, he raised his paw up to Toby and the two dogs began to play.

Just like that!

He sat still on the swing and watched their playful antics. Marshmallow must be feeling better, thought Justin. He'd been so sad and quiet after his sister died. Justin continued to watch the dogs play, but before long Drake, who was no match for the faster, more energetic puppy, stopped frolicking and lay down in the grass to rest. Toby, still filled with energy, tried to provoke the older dog to play more, but Drake refused to budge. Justin decided to get the black ball he had bought for Toby on their trip. Like Toby, Drake loved to play ball.

"I'll be back in a minute, guys," Justin said to the dogs as he ran past them. He closed the gate securely behind him and ran up the deck stairs and through the back door. The kitchen was empty.

"Ma!" his voice echoed through the house.

"I'm upstairs!" his mother yelled down to him.

Justin took the stairs two at a time and burst into his parents' bedroom where his mother was unpacking from the trip.

"Do you know where the black ball is that I bought for Toby?" he asked.

"I thought you put it in your suitcase. Did you unpack yet?"

"Kind of."

"I bet that's where it is," his mother said. "And don't forget, when Jessica and your father get back from the park, we're going over to Aunt Sarah's, so be ready to go."

"I know, Ma. I'll be ready."

Justin ran into his room. The suitcase he had used on the trip lay open in the corner of his room surrounded by scattered clothes. He remembered putting the ball in the large pocket on the outside of the suitcase. Bending down, he stuck his hand in the slot and swept it back and forth. His hand hit the ball in the corner.

Justin ran back outside holding the ball. Drake noticed the toy first and raised himself up off the ground. Toby followed the older dog's lead, thinking Drake wanted to play again. But when he saw the ball in Justin's hand, he gave a sharp yelp and ran to the boy. Justin held the ball out and led the dogs into an open area of the yard. Toby danced around his legs, eagerly anticipating the game that was about to begin. With the dogs' attention riveted to the ball in his hand, Justin tossed it a short distance. Drake, the more experienced of the two, reached the ball first and brought it back to Justin. Justin threw it again, a little harder, and this time Drake beat Toby to the ball again, but by a smaller margin. After a few more throws, Toby was easily beating Drake to the ball. Justin tried to think of a way to make the game fairer for Drake. He was just about to toss the ball in Drake's direction, when he heard a door slam shut. He turned toward the house and saw his mother standing on the deck.

"Justin," she called out. "Lunch time!"

"Okay, Mom. I'll be right there." He turned back to the dogs. "Okay you two, I want you to play and get to know each other. Drake, you're the oldest, so you're in charge. Make sure nothing happens to Marshmallow." He patted both dogs on the head and ran to the house, leaving them lying on the grass next to the swing.

✧   ✧   ✧

DRAKE WAS TIRED. He hadn't exercised much during his stay at the kennel. The aides had taken him for a short walk twice a day, but the pace was always leisurely, too slow to be considered real exercise—not that Drake could go very fast with his limp. As he rested in the cool grass, he looked over at Toby. He was curious about the puppy, who looked no more than five or six months old.

"What happened to your leg?" Toby asked Drake.

"It's an old injury. When I was a puppy, maybe a little older than you, I broke my leg. The bones never healed properly."

"How did it happen?" Toby asked; his head cocked. Having a friend like Drake would be nice, he thought, as he awaited the older dog's response. He couldn't imagine becoming friends with Meesha and Pinka.

Drake hesitated. Though the memory of the incident had faded over time along with the fear and horror of what had happened, Toby's innocent question took him by surprise and some of the old feelings began to surface.

"As I said, when I was about your age . . . How old are you, Toby?"

"Four months old."

"You're big for your age."

"I was the biggest of my siblings," Toby said. "My sister, Tara, was smaller, though."

"You have a sister?"

Toby hadn't meant to mention his sister. The comment had just slipped out. The older dog was so easy to talk to that his guard had dropped. The grief that he had been struggling to keep at bay, crashed down on him again.

Drake could tell something bad must have happened to Toby's sister by his reaction to the question. Something recent that was still fresh for the young dog; something time had not yet worked its healing powers on. Drake, having been through his own emotional adversity, knew not to push Toby further.

"You don't have to talk about what happened, Toby," Drake said softly. "Someday, if you want to tell me about it, you can." Drake paused for a moment.

Toby was grateful Drake didn't press him about Tara. He couldn't talk about what had happened yet; the memory of her death was still too painful.

Just then, the kitchen door slammed shut, interrupting their conversation. Both dogs turned to see the boy running toward them. Toby would have to wait to hear Drake's story.

CHAPTER 19

RAY CLOSED THE mailbox flap and pressed the button on the garage door opener attached to his car visor. Once inside the garage, he pushed the button again, and the door closed noisily behind him. Lisa's car was gone. For a moment, Ray wondered where she might have gone. Then he remembered. During breakfast she had mentioned that she was planning to take Justin and Jessica shopping for more clothes for the new school year, which had started two weeks earlier. The summer sure went by fast, Ray thought as he grabbed his briefcase from the passenger seat and went into the house.

He placed the large black case on the kitchen floor and sifted through the mail for the credit card bill. The envelope he was looking for wasn't there. He set the stack of mail back on the kitchen table. Just then he heard the garage door open again, and a few moments later, Justin and Jessica burst into the house with shopping bags in their hands. Lisa followed behind them, carrying more bags.

"Hi, guys!" said Ray. "You had a successful trip, huh?"

"Yeah! You should see the great shirts and cool jeans Ma bought for me," Justin said, as he pulled the jeans out of the bag and held them up for his father to see.

"Do you want to know what I got, Daddy?" Jessica asked.

"I sure do."

"I got a new dress and skirt and sweater," Jessica took a breath, "and hair ties and a pair of shoes."

"Great!" said Ray. He went over and gave Lisa a kiss hello. "Did you buy anything for yourself?" he asked her, as he walked over to the refrigerator and opened the door.

Lisa took off her jacket. "No, I didn't have time to look for myself." She hung her jacket on a hook next to the garage door. "By the way, I had to write a check for the kids' clothes. The credit card wouldn't go through. Is there enough money in the account to cover the check?"

Ray's body stiffened and his stomach flip-flopped. The idea that Lisa might use the credit card to buy the school clothes hadn't occurred to him. How stupid of him! He continued to examine the contents of the refrigerator to avoid her eyes.

"Ray, did you hear me?"

"Oh, yeah. How much did the bill come to?"

"A little over two hundred dollars."

"No problem. There's more than enough in the account to cover that."

Lisa set her pocketbook down on the table next to the pile of mail. "Why do you think the credit card wouldn't go through?" she asked. "Did you pay the bill?"

Ray turned to face Lisa. "I'm pretty sure I did. I'll double-check my records," he said, and stuck his head back in the refrigerator. "Maybe their computer system messed up. It's probably something like that." He grabbed a can of soda and shut the refrigerator door.

"All right," Lisa said. "But let me know, okay? I was pretty embarrassed when the clerk told me the purchase was denied. I'm glad I had the checkbook with me."

"Sure, I'll let you know," Ray said. He picked his briefcase up off the floor and left the kitchen. I have to be more careful, he thought as he entered his office. He shook his head and set the briefcase on his desk.

The next day Lisa called her friend Tracy, who worked at the Humane Society. Things had been so hectic, it was the first chance she had to call her since they arrived back home. Tracy was excited to hear about the new puppy, and they made plans for her to stop by after work that day to see him.

Lisa had met Tracy when Drake was a puppy. She had been the instructor at Drake's training class and had given Lisa and Drake extra attention because of his disability. Tracy had a special relationship with animals; they all loved her, and Drake was no exception. When Tracy discovered she lived only a couple of blocks away from Lisa, she insisted they get together. It wasn't long before they became best friends.

Lisa went into the kitchen and poured herself another cup of coffee. She had heard the mail truck stop by earlier, and though Ray usually picked up the mail when he came home from work, today she decided to get it; any excuse to step out into the fresh autumn day.

A gust of cool wind buffeted her when she opened the front door. The air whipped her hair about her face as she walked to the mailbox at the edge of the street. She pulled the edges of her cardigan sweater tightly together.

Back in the house, Lisa sat down at the kitchen table and shuffled through the usual stack of envelopes and sorted them into piles: one for the business, one for bills, and one for junk mail. The last envelope was the credit card bill. Slipping her index finger under the loose end of the flap she quickly pulled it down the length of the envelope and took out the folded papers.

As she read the statement, the first thing she noticed was the balance on the account. There must be a mistake, she thought. Our balance can't be this high. The amount listed was over their credit limit! No wonder her purchase had been denied yesterday. She looked down at the itemized section of the bill. Two entries stared back at her, both for the Oasis casino in Las Vegas, and both for $2,500! We didn't go to the Oasis casino, thought Lisa. There has to be a mistake. Maybe Ray lost his credit card while we were there and someone used it. She'd better call them right away.

As she dialed the phone, an uneasy thought entered her mind. What if Ray was the one who made the charges? He hadn't said anything to her about losing his card. But when did he have the opportunity to go to a casino? The only time they weren't together was when he was golfing.

"Hello, may I have your account number please?" the woman at the other end of the phone asked.

Lisa read off the charge account number from the bill in her hand and waited during a brief pause.

"Mrs. Johnson?"

"Yes."

"How may I help you?"

"I just received a bill in the mail today, and there are two cash advances from when we were in Las Vegas, each for $2,500. We didn't take any money out against this account while we were there."

"Hold on one moment while I check to see who signed for the charges."

Lisa waited for what seemed an interminable time.

"Raymond Johnson signed for the charges at the Oasis casino. Is that your husband?"

"Yes, but I'm not aware that he made any charges for those amounts."

"Have you asked him about the charges yet?"

"No, he isn't home."

"I recommend you talk to him first before I put the account in a lost or stolen card status. Once that occurs, you have to be reissued a new account number and card. I don't see any other charges since then. Oh, I'm sorry, there was a purchase denied yesterday for an over-limit card use attempt."

"That was me. I wanted to use the card to buy some school clothes for the kids."

"Well, if you find your husband didn't make those charges, call us back right away so we can put a stop on the account. Someone is available twenty-four hours a day at the number you dialed."

"Okay. Thanks for your help." Lisa slowly placed the telephone handset back on the hook. If Ray did make those charges, what did he spend the money on, and when did he have the chance to spend it? Suddenly Lisa remembered the two red chips she had found in his pants pocket when she had done the laundry from the trip. She had initially thought they had something to do with golfing. A sinking feeling overtook her. She slowly sat down in the kitchen chair next to where she stood.

Ray turned down the street and pulled the car up to the mail box. When he pulled down the flap, he saw the box was empty.

"Uh-oh," he said. Lisa must have picked up the mail. It never came this late, and he couldn't remember the last time they hadn't received *any* mail. He prayed the credit card bill hadn't come, and if it had, that she hadn't opened it yet.

Ray immediately knew something was wrong. Lisa sat at the kitchen table; her face was pale. Next to her, on the table, was an open envelope with several pieces of paper lying next to it.

"Hi, hon," he said, and bent down to give her a kiss. She turned her head away from him. Ray was now close enough to recognize the credit card statement on the table. Next to the paper were two familiar red poker chips.

Lisa slowly turned her head toward Ray and looked up at him. She still didn't speak. When she finally spoke, she selected her words carefully.

"I need you to be completely honest with me, Ray." Her dark brown eyes bore into his. He wanted to look away, but he couldn't. Her eyes held his. He didn't need to answer her. She knew he was guilty.

"What did you spend the money on?" she asked quietly

and calmly. The charade was over. She had found out about the money he had lost and that was that. There was nothing he could do to change that fact now. The only question left was what would happen next. Lisa sat there and calmly watched him. It was the calm before the storm, Ray was certain of that. She spoke again.

"How are we going to pay for this, Ray?" Her voice became louder, angrier.

Ray still didn't respond. He turned away. He couldn't look at her anymore.

"Five thousand dollars. Five thousand dollars!" Her voice was almost a screech as she repeated the amount. "How could you have done this? What were you thinking? Is all of the money gone?"

Ray just stood there staring at his wife.

"Answer me!"

"Yes," he responded.

The pressure released in Lisa. "You gambled away five thousand dollars without even mentioning it to me?" she yelled at him. "Did you think I wouldn't find out?"

At that moment something in Ray snapped. Why did he have to answer to her? He wasn't a child. She wasn't his father, who up until he had left them had used fear to rule his family. The old familiar beast, which had been dormant so long, began to swell inside Ray. As the rage inside him grew, he knew there was only one thing that could extinguish it.

The door to the garage slammed shut. Lisa heard the car start and the rattling of the garage door as it rose. She waited to hear the door shut again, but no sound followed. Instead, she heard the sharp squealing of tires protesting against pavement as the car sped down the street.

"Oh, God," she said, and clasped her head with her hands. The kitchen clock ticked boldly against the still silence of the house. The children would be home from school any minute. Lisa knew she had to pull herself together before they arrived. She raised her head and gathered the papers scattered on the table. Where had Ray gone? She hadn't seen him that furious since his last drinking binge several years ago, and he had come too far to go back to that, hadn't he? Lisa dismissed the thought. She refused to consider that the nightmare might begin all over again.

CHAPTER 20

TOBY AND DRAKE quickly became best of friends. They spent their mornings annoying the cats or following the woman as she went about her chores. Sometimes they just lay on the living room rug talking and relaxing. In the afternoon when the boy came home from school, he would take them outside and play ball with them or sit on the old swing and watch the two play.

Toby hadn't brought up the subject of Drake's maimed leg since the first day he had arrived at the house, and Drake hadn't brought up the subject of Tara to Toby. Toby knew the time would come when he would open his heart to Drake. Thoughts of Tara were not as painful as they had been. His preoccupation with his new home and family gave him the time he needed to start the healing process, and he began to slowly rise out of the quagmire of his grief.

One evening after the cats had gone outside for their nightly escapades and Drake had fallen asleep, Toby went into the kitchen for a drink of water. As he left the kitchen to go back the living room, a pale moonbeam streaming through one of the windows caught his eye. The dim ray cast its translucent light onto the bottom half of the back door. In the center of the frame of light, the outline of the cat door stood out. Curiosity consumed him. Could he go outside like the cats did? Would he fit through the flap? Toby knew he should go straight back to his corner and ignore his curiosity, but the contest between his inquisitiveness and good sense was easily won by the former.

Toby walked over to the dark flap. He tentatively pushed his head against it the way the cats did when they went outside. The thick rubber cover gave way to the pressure, but did not open completely. Toby pushed again, harder this time, and suddenly he found himself outside on the deck. He stood there for a moment in surprise. The night was dark and quiet.

Moonlight cast mottled shadows on the ground where the more persistent beams filtered through the thick foliage of the old oak tree. Even with the moonlight, it was too dark to see much. There was no sign of Meesha or Pinka or any other living creatures in the area. He began to panic. What if he couldn't get back in the house? His heart pounded in his ear. He turned around and pushed his head against the flap. Once more the rubber yielded to the pressure, and he was back inside.

He was halfway across the kitchen floor, when a bright flash blinded him. His young eyes adjusted quickly to the unexpected illumination. The man stood between him and the opening to the living room.

✧ ✧ ✧

THE MOOD IN THE house was sullen and tense. Lisa and Ray had barely spoken since their confrontation two days earlier. Something would have to give soon; the atmosphere affected the children. Justin had asked his mother why they were mad at each other, but Lisa hadn't answered him.

She knew Ray had been drinking again. The past two evenings after supper he had ensconced himself in his office until the children went to bed. Then he slipped out of the house without a word and didn't return until after one in the morning when he would shut himself in the spare bedroom next to his study to sleep off his drunken stupor. It was an all too familiar pattern Lisa had lived with for years.

She looked at the clock on her nightstand. The large florescent green numbers glared at her. 1:15. He'd be home any time now. Lisa knew she had to take some action, get control of the situation before it was too late, before the damage was irreparable. Tomorrow they would talk.

Ray swore as he stumbled over the door jamb. He recovered and shut the door quietly behind him. He was home later than usual. Friday nights the bars were open until two, and the owner had let Ray and a few of the regulars stay after closing to play a few more games of pool. Hell'uva nice guy, Ray thought. He had a few more drinks than usual, too. And he was hungry. Awkwardly, he felt his way through the dark living room. Ray didn't want to risk waking Lisa by turning the light on. Their bedroom was at the top of the stairs. He had left the car parked in the driveway so the sound of the garage door opening wouldn't wake her.

When he reached the opening to the kitchen, he ran his hand up and down the wall where he expected to find the light switch. The smoothness of the wall was uninterrupted. Where the hell was the switch? Did someone move the stupid thing? He continued to feel along the wall until his fingers touched the edge of the switch plate. A moment later the light flashed on. He closed his eyes to the stinging brightness and rubbed them with his finger tips.

Once his eyes adjusted to the light, Ray started toward the refrigerator, but something on the floor caught his attention. It's that stupid puppy. What was his name? Marshmallow, that's right. What kind of name is that for a dog anyway?

"What are you doing in here?" Ray slurred his words as he spoke. "I never should have let 'em keep you. What good are you anyway? I'm glad your stupid sister died. Too bad you didn't follow her example," Ray grumbled. The puppy turned and ran under the table.

"You think you can get away from me, huh?" Ray ambled unsteadily to the table and clumsily dropped onto his hands and knees. "No dog is going to get the best of me." He stretched his hand under the table, but his reach was a foot or so short of where Toby cowered. Ray realized he'd have to actually crawl under the table to grab hold of the dog. That would be too much trouble to go to for some stupid mutt. He gave up and pushed himself up off the floor. Just as Ray steadied himself, Toby ran out from under the table. The motion startled Ray, but he quickly recovered and lunged forward, grabbing the puppy before he could slip by. He stood up with the dog firmly in his grip. Once erect, he raised Toby to his face.

"You're in for it now, you stupid mutt! No one gets the best of Ray Johnson." He violently shook Toby and threw him down on the hard tile floor. Before Toby could get up, Ray kicked him several feet across the floor. Toby let out a yelp of pain.

"Shut up you, stupid mutt!" Ray pulled his leg back again and swung his foot at Toby even harder this time, but Toby managed to get up and move far enough away so that Ray's boot only grazed his back hip. Ray swore. How could he miss the stupid thing? As he positioned himself to swing his foot again, Ray heard a deep growl coming from the direction of the living room and turned toward the doorway.

Drake stood in the opening, his teeth bared.

Ray couldn't believe the dog was growling at him! In his own house!

Forgetting Toby for a moment, Ray turned to face Drake. The dog's growling continued, and the fur on his back stood on end. For the first time since they had gotten the dog, Ray found himself afraid of the animal. The fear partially sobered him. His hands began to shake. He felt silly, a grown man cowering before a dog. His pride forced him to look down at the white puppy now huddled under the table.

"I guess I'll have to take care of you some other time when your bodyguard isn't around," Ray said. He tried to sound intimidating, but his voice shook. All he wanted to do was run. But instead, he turned and slowly made his way down the hallway, the eyes of the two dogs fixed on his back.

✧　✧　✧

TOBY COULDN'T STOP trembling. He had never been so scared and in so much pain before. I wonder if this is how Tara felt, he thought. The pain had been bad when he hit the floor after the man threw him, but that was nothing compared to the excruciating pain he felt in his leg. Thankfully, the man had only grazed him on his second attempt. Toby wondered if he'd be able to walk back to his bed.

Drake peered under the rounded edge of the table; his expression was mixed with fear and concern. "Toby, are you okay?" he asked tremulously. Adrenalin still coursed through his body, filling him with equal amounts of rage and fear. Fear for his young friend. Rage at the man.

Toby looked up. Drake had saved his life. The man would certainly have killed him if Drake hadn't been there.

Toby answered slowly, his voice shaking. "I don't know. My leg really hurts. I think he might have broken it."

Drake froze. The memory of his own experience with the man flashed before him. He pushed the weight of it out of his mind.

"Do you think you can walk back to your bed?" Drake tried to keep the panic he felt out of his voice. Though no place in the house was safe from the man's wrath, it would be easier to keep watch from there.

"I'll try," Toby said, and attempted to get up on his

three good legs. After struggling for a moment, he managed to stand, but the pain in his left rear leg was too severe to support any weight. Toby started forward holding his injured leg in the air. Progress was slow, but he managed to hobble into the living room and back to his corner. Drake curled up on the carpet next to Toby's bed. He had no intention of leaving his friend's side.

"What happened, Toby?"

"I went in the kitchen to get a drink of water. Then the man came in and surprised me. I didn't hear him. The light went on and there he was. I tried to get away from him, but . . ." He didn't tell Drake about his trip out the cats' door. Drake would be angry with him. If he hadn't taken the time to go outside he wouldn't have encountered the man.

"You have to be more careful," Drake gently admonished Toby. "Especially now that he's mad at you. We have to stay together at all times. Something's wrong with him. He's been acting like he used to years ago. I don't know what happened, but we'll have to be vigilant." Drake would have to tell Toby what the man had done to him so many years ago. He owed his little friend that much, but it could wait until another day. For now, Toby needed his rest.

✧　✧　✧

IT DIDN'T FIT. Why would a dog be growling at a Christmas party? And just before that, she could have sworn she had heard a yelp of some kind. Lisa continued to mill around the party and mix with her old coworkers. But the growling persisted and the incongruity of the events slowly stirred her out of her dream and into consciousness.

She opened her eyes and sat up in bed. The house was quiet. A light was on downstairs. Ray must be home, she thought. I must have heard him come in while I slept. She lay back down, but she couldn't shake the feeling that something was wrong. I must have been dreaming about something unpleasant, she thought, and tried to recollect the subject of her dream, but the details eluded her, and she drifted back to sleep.

CHAPTER 21

JUSTIN JUMPED OUT of bed. Today was the day his mother had promised they could take the dogs hiking at the state park near where they lived. He quickly made his bed and threw on a pair of jeans and an old sweatshirt. The muted sound of the television in the family room drifted up into his bedroom as it did every Saturday morning. Cartoons didn't interest Justin anymore.

He sat on the edge of the bed and quickly put on his sneakers. As he left the room, he grabbed his blue baseball cap off the hook by the door and plopped it backward on his head. He ran down the stairs to the family room where he expected to find the two dogs with his sister. He didn't notice them both lying in Toby's corner as he flew through the living room and down the hall. Jessica sat on the floor in her pajamas a few feet from the television. The dogs weren't with her.

Justin went back to the living room. Drake's corner, the first one he could see as he rounded the corner, was empty. He began to panic until he saw both dogs lying in Toby's corner.

"What's going on, guys? You decided to sleep together last night, huh?" Drake got up and slowly moved toward Justin.

"Hi, boy." Justin went over and greeted the old dog with a pat on his head. Drake looked up and licked Justin's hand several times.

"Let's wake up Marshmallow." Justin went over to Toby. The puppy's eyes slowly opened and sorrowfully gazed at Justin. Toby usually ran to Justin as soon as he saw him, but this time he just lay there, still and quiet.

"What's the matter, Marshmallow? It's time to get up. Come on, we're going for a hike today," Justin encouraged the puppy. But Toby still didn't move. He bent down and started to pick up the puppy, but as soon as he raised him off the ground, Toby let out a yelp. Justin immediately placed him back down. Marshmallow's hurt! Without stopping to wonder what had happened, he turned and ran up the stairs two at a time calling for his mother. He leapt onto the landing and began pounding on his parents' bedroom door.

"Ma! Ma!" he called out, but there was no answer. He opened the door and ran into the room. The bed was empty, his father's side still made. He heard the sound of water running behind the master bathroom door.

"Ma! Marshmallow's hurt!" he yelled, as he pounded on the door.

"What, Justin? I can't hear you. I'll be out in a minute," his mother called back to him. The water stopped running.

"Marshmallow's hurt!" Justin yelled again. "He can't stand up!" The door to the bathroom flew open, and Lisa rushed out in her bathrobe, her wet hair dripping onto the soft velour.

"Marshmallow's hurt? What's wrong with him?" she asked, as she frantically tightened the sash of her robe and pushed the wet mass of hair out of her face.

"I don't know. He was just lying there. When I went to pick him up, he cried out."

Lisa ran down the stairs with Justin behind her. Jessica sat on the floor next to Toby.

"What's wrong with Marshmallow, Mommy?" she asked.

"I don't know, honey. Move over so I can take a look at him." Jessica stood up and moved to the side.

Lisa gently stroked Toby on the head as she tried to discern what was wrong. She let her palm run down his back and then carefully put her hands under each side of his stomach and slowly raised him. His legs started to hang down, and she slowly released him. As the weight of his body transferred from her hands to his legs, she noticed that he held his left rear leg up as if he were afraid to put any weight on it.

"Something's wrong with his leg," Lisa said, puzzled. "I wonder what happened. Did he hurt himself yesterday when you were playing outside with him?" she asked Justin.

"No. He was fine all day. This is the first time I've seen him act like this."

"We'd better take him to the vet. You two stay here with him while I go call the animal hospital." Lisa stood up and rushed into the kitchen. She paged through the small address book they kept near the telephone on the kitchen counter.

Suddenly, she froze.

A fragment of her dream from the night before popped into her head. She was at a Christmas party at work, and there was a small yelp and the sound of a dog growling. She remembered waking up and thinking how odd that was. She had forgotten that she had woken up at all, but now the event came back to her in a rush of clarity. She had assumed Ray entering the house had stirred her from her sleep, but now she realized it had been the dog sounds. Had they been part of her dream, or had the sounds been real? Ray had been home when she woke up; the light downstairs was on. Did he hurt Marshmallow? Her breathing quickened. Her shoulder muscles tensed. He better not have. She would confront him later. Right now, she needed to get the puppy to a vet.

"Ma, is Marshmallow going to be all right?" Jessica asked. The pet carrier holding Toby sat between Justin and his sister on a smooth wooden bench against the wall of the animal hospital's waiting room.

"He'll be fine, Jessica. The doctor just needs to examine him to make sure."

"But the doctor checked Fluffy to make sure she was okay, and she died."

Lisa looked over at her daughter. Kids didn't miss a thing. "I know, honey, but that doesn't mean Marshmallow's going to die."

"Ma," Justin said, "did you notice that it's the same leg Drake hurt when he was a puppy?"

Lisa thought for a moment. Justin was right. It was the

same leg. The left leg. A sense of dread coursed through her.

A young woman wearing a light-blue smock walked into the waiting room with a manila folder in her hand.

"Marshmallow?" she asked.

"Right here," Lisa answered. She stood and picked up the pet carrier. The young woman smiled and beckoned the small group to follow her down a brightly lit hallway.

"I'm going to have you go into examination room three. The doctor will be with you in a moment." She led them into a small, sterile white room, then left and shut the door. Lisa set the carrier on the metal examination table.

"Do you think Marshmallow's leg is broken?" Justin asked his mother.

"I don't know. I hope not." At that moment the door opened and Dr. Carlson entered the room. He had been their veterinarian for the past ten years. "Hi Lisa! Hi kids! What do we have here, a new addition to the family?"

Justin spoke up first. "We just got him. His name is Marshmallow."

Dr. Carlson opened the door to the carrier and peeked in at the puppy.

"You're a handsome guy," he cooed. He looked over at Lisa. "When you called you told the receptionist one of his legs was hurt. Which one?"

"The left back leg."

"How did it happen?"

"We don't know. He was fine when we went to bed last night, but this morning Justin discovered he was hurt when he went to pick him up." She hesitated a moment. Should she tell him about the yelp she thought she heard during the night? She decided not to.

Dr. Carlson turned back to his patient. "Well, little guy, let's find out what's bothering you." He carefully took Toby out of the carrier and gently set him on the table while keeping his hands under the puppy's stomach for support. Toby stood with his left rear leg just touching the table as the doctor examined it.

"I don't think the leg's broken, but let's have some x-rays taken just to be sure. It's probably a bad bruise or sprain. The x-rays will only take a few minutes. You might be more comfortable waiting in the front room. I'll have my assistant call you back in after I've reviewed them."

Dr. Carlson left the room with Toby. Lisa and the kids headed back to the waiting room. Once there, Jessica asked her mother if she could go look in the small store where they sold pet food and kept the animals that were up for adoption. She wanted to look at the kittens. Lisa assented and sat down on the wooden bench next to Justin.

"Ma," Justin said after Jessica was out of earshot.

"Yes, Justin?"

"Do you think Dad knows what happened to Marshmallow?"

The question startled Lisa. She looked at her son in silence for a moment. Where did that come from? "What makes you ask that?"

This time it was Justin who hesitated. He glanced toward the store where Jessica stood by the cages that housed the kittens. He looked down at his sneakers and then said, "If I ask you something, will you tell me the truth?"

"Of course," she responded immediately, and then wondered if she should have agreed so readily. He sounded serious. "What is it, Justin?"

He paused for several moments, then turned to his mother and asked, "Was Dad the one who broke Prince's leg when he was a puppy?" His soft brown eyes looked at her for the truth. She looked away. How long had Justin suspected his father? What had brought about his suspicions? Maybe he had overheard her talking about what had happened when he was younger. Children understand more than adults realize, she thought. How much should she tell him? What will he think of his father if I tell him the truth? Over the years she had tried to shield the children from their father's drinking and the violent episodes that sometimes followed. For the most part, she thought she had succeeded.

Justin interrupted her thoughts. "Did he hurt him when he was drunk?"

Now came Lisa's turn to look down at the floor. She couldn't lie to him. Somehow he already knew the answers to the questions he found so hard to ask.

She looked back at her son. He waited for her response.

"Yes, Justin," she admitted to him. "He did. I'm sorry."

"It's not your fault, Ma. I know Dad wouldn't have done something like that if he hadn't been drinking." Justin waited a moment, then asked, "Dad's drinking again, isn't he?"

Lisa was taken aback at her son's compassion and perception. When had he grown up so much? She risked alienating him if she weren't honest with him.

"Yes, Justin, he is. He goes out at night after you and Jessica are asleep."

"I know," Justin replied. "I hear the car start up when he

leaves, and sometimes I wake up when he comes home."

Lisa didn't know what to say. She felt the need to apologize to her son for his father's alcoholism, for Prince's broken leg, and now, for Marshmallow's injury.

"Do you think he hurt Marshmallow last night?" he asked solemnly.

Before Lisa could answer, Dr. Carlson's assistant came into the waiting room to usher them back to the examination room. Jessica reluctantly left the store when Lisa called her to join them. Dr. Carlson had Toby on the table next to the pet carrier.

"I have good news. The x-rays were fine. I didn't see any fractures or breaks. He's a lucky little guy."

"Thank goodness!" Lisa exclaimed.

Justin jumped up and stood next to Toby. Lisa could sense the relief her son felt. "You're going to be okay, Marshmallow," Justin lovingly reassured him.

"I'm not going to put a leg brace on him. Animals are good at taking care of themselves when they're injured, better than most people. He'll start using the leg a little bit at a time as it begins to heal. He should be completely healed in a couple of weeks." Dr. Carlson carefully picked up Toby and placed him back in the carrier. "Where did you get this little guy? He's unusual; especially his tail. He's definitely part German Shepherd, I'm just not sure what the other part is."

Lisa briefly described how Toby had come to them.

"That's quite a story," Dr. Carlson commented after Lisa finished. "He's lucky he ended up with such a good family. Did he have his shots in California?"

"No. We decided to wait until we came home," said Lisa.

"I just haven't gotten around to making an appointment yet. Then this happened."

"Well, he's been through enough today. I'm not going to give them to him now, but I would like to see him for a follow-up in a couple of weeks, and he can get his shots then. Be sure to make an appointment with the receptionist before you leave."

Lisa assured him that she would.

CHAPTER 22

RAY ROLLED OVER onto his side. He reluctantly opened his eyes, and then quickly closed them again. The sun blazed through the small window in his study. He must have forgotten to lower the shade the night before. What time is it? he wondered, and turned his head to peer at the clock on the wall. Almost eleven. A dull ache he hadn't noticed before began to throb in his right temple. He wished he could stay in bed all day, but he had a lot of work to catch up on. Piles of paper threatened to topple out of the wire basket on his desk. He would have to spend the whole day—what was left of it anyway—working. The ache in his head throbbed harder.

The Schaeffer account was his biggest worry. Payment of their claim was overdue. Recently, they had submitted a claim when heavy rains had caused the roof to leak in the company's warehouse and almost $50,000 in equipment had been damaged. Several of the messages on Ray's answering machine were from the vice president of the company who wanted a check right away.

Ray pushed his body into a sitting position. With his chin on his chest, he rubbed his eyes with his fingertips. The dry taste in his mouth made him gag. His tongue felt swollen and parched. He tried to recollect the events of the night before, but only bits and pieces came back to him, mostly of earlier in the evening at Charlie's. I must have laid a good one on, he thought. How in the hell am I going to get all of this work done?

And he had another problem—Lisa. They hadn't spoken to each other in several days. He knew he was wrong. He shouldn't have become defensive with her, and more important, he should never have spent all of that money gambling. What had he been thinking? If he hadn't stopped in the casino that first day and seen that guy win over ten thousand dollars on the slot machine, he would have gone golfing like he was supposed to. Too late now. The only thing left to do was make it up to her. He would work more hours to get more accounts, and as long as he held onto the Schaeffer account, they'd be okay. But first he'd have to get Lisa to forgive him. And he'd have to give up the booze again, too. He would talk to Lisa that evening, after the kids went to bed.

Ray lifted his head from his hands and slowly stood up from the sofa. He hoped no one was using the bathroom upstairs so he could wash off the drunken stench that adhered to him. After pulling on his pants, he opened the study door and entered the hallway. The house was quiet. No one was home. He passed through one end of the kitchen and into the living room. As he headed to the stairs, he noticed Drake in the corner of the room. A fuzzy memory of the night before crept into his mind. He vaguely remembered the dog growling at him for some reason. He had been afraid the dog was going to attack him. Why was that? he wondered. The details eluded him. He looked in the other corner where the puppy usually slept. The spot was empty.

Lisa was grateful Justin hadn't brought up the unanswered question of how Marshmallow was injured in front of Jessica. But she couldn't keep from mulling it over in her mind. Could Ray have had something to do with Marshmallow's injury? While he was under the influence of alcohol, he was certainly capable of hurting the puppy. That had been proven before. How else could the puppy have been injured? Could he have fallen on his own and hurt himself? Unlikely, she thought.

Later that night, Lisa gathered up her courage and went to the family room to confront Ray. He sat with his back to her watching television in the brown leather recliner. She hesitated in the doorway for a moment. They had a good marriage when he wasn't drinking. Alcohol turned him into a completely different person; not the man she had married.

Lisa was tempted to avoid the conflict that would inevitably ensue; instead, she took a deep breath and entered the room.

As soon as Ray noticed her he muted the sound of the television with the remote control.

"We need to talk, Ray." Lisa stood in front of Ray to one side. To her amazement, he turned off the television and stood up to face her. He reached out and took hold of her hands.

Before Lisa could say anything, he looked into her eyes and held her gaze. "I'm sorry, Lisa. Spending the money without talking to you first was wrong. It was a stupid thing to do. I just wanted to win so I could come back and show you the money. I didn't think you would be mad if I won. But I was wrong, huh?"

Lisa was dumbfounded. He had caught her off guard. She had fully expected another loud, upsetting argument. But here he was, apologizing to her, apparently sincere. There were more issues to deal with, though, so she had to remain firm.

"Yes, Ray, you were wrong. Whether you won or lost isn't the issue. The point is you didn't include me in the decision of how we spend our money."

Ray squeezed her hands slightly tighter. "I'll never do it again, Lisa. I promise." Ray's soft brown eyes, Justin's eyes, pleaded with her for forgiveness. But she couldn't forgive him yet, not completely. Time would be needed for these new wounds of their marriage to heal. And whether they healed or not depended on the larger more serious issue of his drinking.

"What about the drinking, Ray?"

He didn't hesitate. "I'll stop again. I promise. I know I can if you're here to support me."

"Are you willing to get help this time?"

"Yes. Yes, I will. I'll go to an AA meeting this week."

"It's going to take more than one meeting, Ray. You'll have to commit to going on a regular basis."

"I know. I'll go to as many meetings as I need to in order to stop drinking for good." Lisa removed her hands from Ray's, turned, and took a few steps away from him. She wanted to distance herself from what she might hear him say in response to her next question.

She turned back to face him and paused for a moment. "Did you have anything to do with Marshmallow's injury to his leg?"

The memory of the night before struck him like a bolt of lightning before she had even completed the question. He saw his foot going out at the small, white puppy on the floor. Flashes of his encounter with the puppy passed quickly before his mind's eye. But just as quickly, his mind formulated a lie.

"Oh, my God, I forgot. I accidently stumbled over him in the kitchen last night after I got home. He let out a small yelp, but I didn't think he was hurt."

The relief Lisa wanted to feel was held back by the doubts that plagued her. Was he telling the truth? He hadn't missed a beat.

"Dr. Carlson said he'll be okay in a week or two. His leg is hurt. It's not broken though," she quickly added.

"That's good," Ray said with relief. "Justin must be upset, huh?"

"He's fine now. He'll be relieved to know what happened."

Ray turned away, placed the remote on the end table, and gently put his arms around his wife. "I'm glad we had this talk, Lisa. Thanks for giving me a chance. I love you, you know." He softly held her face in his hands as he gave her a kiss.

"I love you, too, Ray," Lisa said, physically giving in to his embrace; but her mind still held nagging doubts.

"TOBY?"

"What, Drake?" Toby shifted his body slightly on the soft towel beneath him. The boy had placed the basket that was now his bed under the rambling branches of the old oak tree in the back yard. Drake sprawled out several feet in front of him on the cool, shady grass. The pain from his injured leg had lessened, but the fear he felt from the night before had not.

"I want to tell you how my leg was broken," Drake continued in a sober tone. "I think it's important for you to know after what happened last night."

Finally, Toby thought, he would learn what happened to Drake. His broken leg had to have something to do with the man. Toby was certain of it. He rested his head on his paws and focused on Drake as the older dog told his story.

"The first few months after the family adopted me, things were great. The man didn't pay much attention to me. Occasionally he would pat my head or say a few words to me, but that was all the interaction we had. After a couple of months, things changed. He changed. He became violent and always seemed angry. I did everything I could to stay out of his way, especially when no one else was home.

"One night I was home by myself. The man had left the house earlier, and the woman and the children had been gone all day. The man came home just before dark. He was acting crazy; walking around the house, talking to himself, banging into walls. I stayed huddled in my corner in hopes he'd forget I was there. After a while his ranting subsided,

and I eventually fell asleep.

"Suddenly, he was standing over me yelling and screaming. I didn't look up; I was too scared. I thought if I ignored him, he would leave. But he didn't. He bent down, grabbed me by the back of my neck and yanked me up to his face. His breath smelled rotten, and his eyes held so much rage I was petrified. The next thing I knew, he let go of me. Right before I hit the floor, he kicked me across the room. When I landed, I heard a crack and an unbearable pain shot through my leg. He came at me again, but just before he reached me, the woman came through the door. When she saw him readying himself to kick me again, she screamed. The man yelled back at her and lumbered out of the house, slamming the door behind him.

"The woman took me to a place where they put a brace on my leg—probably the same place she took you. I wore the device for several weeks and after it was removed my leg felt better, but it was never the same again. That's how my leg was broken, Toby," Drake finished.

Toby stared at Drake in stunned silence. Except for a few parts, the story could be his own. A chill passed through his body, and he began to tremble again. He had to get away from this place; he had to leave it forever. Tara had been right; humans couldn't be trusted. Toby looked away for a moment then looked back at his only friend with sadness in his eyes.

"I don't think I can stay here, Drake. I can't live like this, wondering when he's going to go after me again. I was lucky this time, but the next time I might not be so lucky. And what about you? What if he hurts you again? We should both leave and find another home."

"I can't leave this place, Toby. This is my home." Drake looked away. When he looked back, Toby saw tears gathering in the corners of the older dog's eyes. "I love my family. They've taken good care of me. If I left, it would break their hearts, and mine."

"This place doesn't feel like home to me, Drake," Toby said sadly. "Not anymore. Not after what happened last night."

"But Toby, the man never bothered me again after he broke my leg. In all these years, he never touched me again. So it follows he won't bother you again either."

"I don't know, Drake . . ."

"Just take some time to think about it. Don't do anything rash. You can't go anywhere with your injured leg. Besides, where would you go? How would you get away?"

Toby thought for a moment. "I don't know where I'd go. But I do know I can't live in fear all the time. I'd rather be dead; at least then I'd be with Tara."

Finally, the answer to the question; Toby's sister had died. Drake wondered what had caused her death, but now wasn't the time to probe.

"How will you escape?"

"Through the cat door at night when everyone's asleep."

"The cat door? How do you know you can fit through it?"

"I've tried it already."

"When? I never saw you use it."

Toby looked down. When he raised his head, a look of contrition covered his face. "Last night. I wasn't going to tell you because I thought you'd be mad. After I took a drink of water, I went over to the door and pushed on the flap to see if I could go through the door like the cats do. It was easy. A little push and I was outside, just like that."

"But where will you go?"

"I don't know. Somewhere I don't have to worry about humans hurting me. When I lived on the farm I could go anywhere I wanted without fear. Maybe I'll find another farm to live on."

Drake was tired. The telling of the story had taken a toll on him emotionally and physically. He knew he couldn't talk Toby into changing his mind, not yet. Toby's experience with the man was still too fresh. He just hoped that after a little time his young friend would see things differently; that he would be less emotional, more rational. Drake looked back at Toby.

"Will you promise me one thing, Toby? Promise me you won't make a final decision yet. That you'll wait until your leg heals. Then we'll talk again. If you're still determined to leave, I'll help you any way I can. Okay?"

Toby thought for a moment. Making this promise to Drake would be harmless. He couldn't leave until his leg healed anyway, and he loved the older dog with all his heart. His only family; his only friend.

"Okay. I'll do that for you, Drake," Toby said.

Instant relief filled the older dog's eyes.

There was nothing more to say. Drake laid his head down and closed his eyes. He needed to be alone with his thoughts.

Toby looked out in the distance beyond the fence into the neighboring yards and wondered what kind of life awaited him out in the world.

CHAPTER 23

LISA WIPED HER hands on the towel that hung from the stove door handle. The cloth was warm from the heat of the oven. The cake she was baking for Ray's birthday was his favorite—chocolate with chocolate frosting. She couldn't believe he was forty years old today, November twelfth. Exactly a month after her birthday.

As the timer clicked away the minutes until the cake would be done, Lisa stood at the kitchen sink window and watched the dogs play in the yard with the kids. Marshmallow sure recovered quickly, she thought, after she saw him paw playfully at Drake. Almost two weeks had passed since the incident, and things were much better between her and Ray. As he promised, he wasn't drinking and had attended AA meetings the two previous Monday nights. He had run into a business acquaintance of his, Al Brady, at the last meeting, and he and Ray had exchanged telephone numbers in case they needed support or someone to talk to.

The timer dinged loudly, jarring Lisa out of her reflections. She turned the oven off and tested the cake with a toothpick to see if the inside was done. "Perfect," she declared, and set the cake pan on the stove top. In preparation for the icing, she went to take the butter out of the refrigerator so it could soften while the cake cooled, but the butter compartment was empty. She remembered she had used the last stick of butter when she had made popcorn for the kids the night before. She grabbed her coat from the closet and rapped lightly on Ray's office door. A muffled response came from inside. She opened the door. Ray looked up as she walked in. He appeared tired and defeated. The stress from the past several weeks was etched on his face.

"I'm going out to the store for some butter. Do you need anything?"

"Yeah, I need a new career. Could you pick one up for me, please?" Ray asked. "Just kidding, I don't need anything, thanks."

"Okay. I'll be back shortly. The kids are out back playing with the dogs."

"Sure," he mumbled, as he returned to the pile of work on his desk.

Lisa closed the door quietly and went back into the kitchen for her pocketbook. She was worried about her husband. He didn't look good.

He was going to lose the Schaeffer account. He was certain of it. The one account he couldn't afford to lose. When he had finally returned the vice president's calls, she—Ms. Lindstrom—had been direct and to the point. If the check wasn't in her hand by Thursday, Schaeffer Electronics would take their business elsewhere. Good-bye. Click. Well, Thursday afternoon was here and the check wasn't going to be in Ms. Lindstrom's hands today and probably not tomorrow either. Ray would be lucky if he could get the money to her by the middle of the following week.

He sat at his desk debating whether to call her and tell her of the delay or just wait for her to call him. Either way he was finished. The account was as good as gone. Ray reluctantly reached out and dialed her number. The shrill ring of the phone on the other end of the line blared at him through the speaker.

"Schaeffer Electronics. May I help you?" a young man asked on the other end of the line. Ray picked up the handset and asked for Ms. Lindstrom.

"May I ask who's calling, please?" the voice on the other end courteously inquired.

"Ray Johnson from Johnson Insurance." He hadn't planned what he was going to say. He'd have to wing it, use some of the old Johnson charm on her, if he still had any left at forty.

"One moment, please." A few seconds ticked away.

"This is Ms. Lindstrom." Her voice was curt and held no compromise.

"Ms. Lindstrom, this is Ray Johnson."

"Mr. Johnson. I assume you're calling to tell me the check is ready?"

Here goes, thought Ray. "Well actually, Ms. Lindstrom, I . . ."

"Mr. Johnson," she interrupted, "I'm a busy person. I don't have time to listen to any excuses or contrived stories. Do you or do you not have the check for me? A simple yes or no will do."

Ray hesitated. He felt compelled to give her the litany of excuses he had conjured up, but it wouldn't matter. She was as rigid and cold as steel. Instead of answering her and giving her the opportunity to hang up on him again, he slowly reached out to the base of the telephone and pressed the call release button.

The account was gone.

Despair crept into his veins and flowed through his body. His first reaction was he needed a drink. Just one. Enough to take the edge off. One would be okay, wouldn't it?

Who was he kidding? Of course one wouldn't be okay. He knew that. He had tried many times to stop at one and had never been able to. He thought back to the discussions at the two AA meetings he had attended. Alcohol was a crutch. A way to turn off unpleasant emotions, numb them, bury them, and hope they wouldn't resurface. But they always did sooner or later. And then you would have to drink again. And the battle went on . . . and on . . . and on. That was exactly how Ray had used alcohol. Whenever he had a problem instead of facing the situation, he turned to his friend in the bottle. Who else was there to turn to? Then an idea struck him.

Al.

He could call Al.

Where had he put his number? In his wallet. Ray partially stood up and pulled his wallet out of the back pocket of his pants. He sat back down and rifled through the small pieces of paper he kept in one of the side slots. A yellow piece of paper caught his eye. He unfolded it.

Bingo!

The phone rang twice, and then went directly to voice mail. Ray hadn't expected that. But of course Al wouldn't be home now, he'd be at work. After a brief greeting, the message beep sounded.

"Hi, Al. It's Ray. Just calling to see how you're doing. You don't have to bother calling me back. I'll see you next week at the meeting." Ray hung up the phone. It rang as soon as he let go of the handset. Ray looked at the black handset suspiciously. Al couldn't be calling back so soon. There hadn't been enough time for him to even listen to the message. Ray's answering machine picked up before he could decide whether or not to answer the call. He listened to the message as it recorded.

"Mr. Johnson, this is Tod calling from Schaeffer Electronics. Ms. Lindstrom asked me to contact you to inform you that the company will no longer need your services. You'll receive a letter regarding this matter shortly. Thank you." Silence followed and the answering machine shut off.

So that was that. Ray slammed his fist down on the desk. Who does she think she is? He swept his arm across the top of the desk, pushing everything in its wake over the edge and onto the floor. The large bulging folder labeled "Schaeffer File" caught the corner of the tier of black plastic baskets Ray used to organize his work. They fell over onto the floor with the rest of the papers and writing utensils. Ray watched as the large stack of papers that had been in the top tray fanned apart in the air and scattered on the floor.

"Damn!" Ray swore out loud. His fury escaped again. He

had to get out of the house. He felt as if he were suffocating. His anger pumped adrenaline into his body, and he yanked open the door to the hallway. The smell of chocolate wafted into his nostrils, but even that sensation was devoid of pleasure for him. He stormed into the kitchen. Lisa stood at the counter unpacking groceries from a paper bag. She spun around when Ray exploded into the kitchen.

"What's the matter?" she asked anxiously. Something was very wrong.

"I just lost the Schaeffer account. I have to get out of here. I feel like I can't breathe."

"Ray, wait," Lisa pleaded. "It's not the end of the world. I know it feels like it is, but it isn't. We can survive without the Schaeffer account. You'll get another account to take its place."

He glared angrily at her. "You don't know what you're talking about. You don't understand what that account means to us financially. The account was the largest I had. We can't afford to lose it!" He turned from her and grabbed his jacket off the hook by the door to the garage.

"Where are you going?" she asked, trying to suppress the panic that threatened to spill into her voice.

"I have to get out of here."

"Ray, wait." He stopped on the first step down into the garage. "You're not going to drink, are you? Not after everything we've been through. Please, Ray."

He looked back at her, thinking, why make her suffer too?

"Of course not, I just need to get out of here for awhile."

"Are you going to be home in time for supper? Don't forget we're celebrating your birthday tonight. The kids will be disappointed if you miss dinner. Promise me you'll be back in time . . . and that you'll be sober?"

"Yeah, I'll be back in time," he mumbled, and slammed the door behind him. He jumped in his car and backed out of the garage. Once on the road, he drove around aimlessly, growing more and more despondent. He couldn't deal with the feelings that threatened to strangle him. He didn't know how to. There was only one way he knew of to deal with them, and that was to drink until they were extinguished. A red traffic light loomed up ahead of him. He stopped the car to wait for the light to change and took notice of his surroundings. Well, he thought, I guess it just was meant to be. I'll only have one, he promised himself as he pulled into a parking space in front of the neon lights shining out from the windows of Charlie's Café. But deep inside Ray knew the promise was an empty one.

"Where's Daddy?" Jessica asked, as Lisa placed the dinner plate in front of her daughter on the table. "He's going to miss his birthday dinner."

Avoiding eye contact with Jessica, Lisa continued to put food on Justin's plate. "Your father had some important business to take care of, honey. He wasn't sure what time he'd be home. But he said if he wasn't home by seven, to eat without him, and he'd try to be back in time for dessert."

Jessica wasn't satisfied with her mother's answer. "What if he misses dessert, too?" she asked.

"Well, we'll just have to celebrate his birthday tomorrow night."

"But *today's* his birthday, not *tomorrow*."

"That's okay sweetie, he won't mind," Lisa reassured her. "Now eat your dinner." Lisa had waited until seven o'clock to serve the kids supper in hopes their father would come home.

"But you're not eating," Justin pointed out.

Lisa busied herself at the stove and answered her son without looking at him. "I'm going to wait for your father to get home."

Jessica picked up the fork next to her plate and fidgeted in her chair. Lisa had made a pork roast, Ray's favorite. She poked her fork in a piece of the meat and turned to look at the chocolate cake sitting on the counter, frosted and ready to eat.

"You and Daddy won't eat the cake without us, will you?"

Lisa looked over at her daughter. I wish all my worries were so small, she thought, then replied, "Of course not. If he doesn't come home in time for dessert before you go to bed, we'll have the cake tomorrow night."

"What about the presents and the card we bought him?"

"We'll do all of the celebrating tomorrow night. Now stop worrying, okay?" Lisa opened the refrigerator and took out the milk. "Finish your dinner so if he does come home you'll be done." Just then the telephone rang. She grabbed the handset off the hook.

"Hello?"

A man's voice asked, "Is Ray there?" Lisa didn't recognize the voice. The call was probably business related.

"He's not home right now. May I take a message?"

"My name's Al Brady. I'm a friend of Ray's. When do you expect him back?"

Lisa hesitated, and then said, "I'm not sure . . ."

"The reason I'm calling," he broke her off, "is Ray left me a message earlier when I was at work. He sounded a little upset. Is everything okay?"

Lisa looked over at Justin and Jessica and decided to continue the call in the family room. "Al, can you hold on for a minute?"

"Sure," he replied.

Lisa placed her hand over the telephone's mouthpiece.

"Kids, I'm going to take this call in the family room. Eat your dinner and I'll be back in a few minutes."

After his mother left the room, Justin turned to his sister and said in a low voice, "Something's wrong. Dad always works at home at night, so why would he leave to go to the office to do work, especially on his birthday?"

Jessica looked at him oddly. If her mother said her father was working, then he was. The thought never occurred to her not to believe what her mother told her.

"I don't know," she responded indifferently, pushing her food back and forth across her plate. Right now she was worried about finishing her supper so she could have a piece of cake.

Abruptly Justin stood up from the table. "Well, I want to find out what's going on," he said, and started toward the hall that led to the family room.

"Where are you going?" Jessica asked.

"Shh!" Justin put his index finger to his lips. "I'm going to find out who Ma's talking to and whether the call has anything to do with Dad."

"I'm coming, too," Jessica declared, and pushed her chair back from the table. Justin reached her just as she stood up.

"No. You stay here. I'll tell you if I hear anything. If we both go we'll get caught. Besides, you haven't even started eating yet. Ma's gonna be mad if she comes back and you haven't touched your food."

Jessica sat back down in the chair and watched her brother slowly move down the hallway until he was out of sight. She looked down at her dinner, picked up several pieces of pork with her fingers, and dropped them on her brother's plate.

Justin moved quietly down the hall. The family room door was open at the other end. His mother's voice was still too distant to distinguish her words. He'd have to move closer. Staying flat against the left wall, he made his way to the bathroom opening. That would be the best place to listen from; if she discovered him there, he could just say he needed to use the bathroom. But when he reached the bathroom doorway, he still couldn't make out what she was saying. He gathered his courage and edged up to the door frame of the family room. Now he could hear her clearly, even though she spoke quietly.

"I'm concerned, Al," Justin heard her say.

Who was Al? Justin had never heard that name before.

"I know," she continued. "I'm trying, but it's happened so many times before and this is the worst thing that's happened to his business in years. He blames himself, as well he should. He let his work slide when he started drinking again. The consequences are catching up with him now." She paused for a moment.

"I don't know. I just hope he doesn't end up down at Charlie's. If I didn't have to stay home with the kids, I'd go down there and look for him. At least then I'd know." Another pause. "Would you? That would be a huge help." And still another pause. "Sure, I'll be here. Thanks, Al." Silence, then the small beep of the telephone off button being depressed.

Justin quickly moved back up the hallway to the kitchen. As soon as he reached the table, Jessica asked him what happened.

"Shh, Ma's coming," he said, as he hastily sat down in his chair and began eating. "I'll tell you later."

Justin stabbed his fork into the pile of pork on his plate and stuffed the pieces in his mouth. He was too busy thinking about the conversation he had overheard to notice the pile was substantially larger than when he had left.

His mother had lied to them. Their father wasn't out working; she didn't know where he was, though she had mentioned Charlie's, whoever he was. She was worried he was out drinking. And this person, Al, had offered to look for his father. Justin would make up something to tell Jessica. She was too young to understand what was going on. He'd tell her a salesperson had called trying to sell them magazines. She'd believe whatever he told her.

Lisa shut off the television and set the remote on the end table.

Nine-thirty.

Al had called to tell her he had found Ray at Charlie's, but that was over an hour ago. Where was he now? She rose from the recliner and started to pace. Her ears were alert to every sound—every creak and groan of the house, every car that went by. She concentrated on the noises as she waited for his car to pull into the driveway. In her single-minded absorption, she didn't notice Drake and Toby enter the room.

The clock ticked away on the fireplace mantel. She thought a cup of tea might calm her and headed to the kitchen. Halfway down the hall, she heard the garage door open. Finally, he was home.

A loud crash followed.

The house shuddered.

What was that?

A car door slammed shut. She hurried down the rest of the hall to the door to the garage. As she reached for the knob, the door flew open, pushing her into the opposite wall. When she recovered from the impact, she found herself face-to-face with Ray.

✧   ✧   ✧

THE MAN WAS gone. The children were asleep upstairs. The woman was in the family room.

"Toby," Drake said.

"Yeah?"

"Let's go keep the woman company. She seems pretty upset about something."

Toby didn't like the idea of being in a room where the man spent so much time.

"Come on," Drake prompted. "She might feel better if she's not alone." Toby reluctantly succumbed to Drake's persuasion.

With Toby in tow, Drake led the way to the family room. The woman stood with her back to them, her hands stuffed in the large pockets of her bathrobe. Abruptly she took a few steps, stopped, turned, and walked back, her head down in deep thought. After a few moments, she repeated her actions. Drake and Toby might as well have been invisible.

Drake walked over and stood several feet from where the woman continued the steady pattern of her revolving journey. After a few moments, Drake walked back to Toby and whispered, "Something bad must have happened. She's really upset." Drake turned a complete circle and settled down on the floor where he could keep his eye on her. Toby lay down next to him.

"I wonder what happened?" he said to Drake.

"I don't know," Drake replied, "but I don't think she even knows we're here." As if to prove Drake's point, the woman abruptly walked out of the room.

Drake slowly rose from the floor. "I guess we should go back to our beds in case the man comes home."

Toby couldn't have agreed more and fell behind Drake as they left the room and started down the hallway. Before they were halfway to the living room, the all-too-familiar sound of the man arriving home trembled throughout the house; seconds later, a loud crash followed. Farther down the hall, Drake saw the woman stop at the door that led to the garage. The man would come through at any moment. There was no time for them to reach the living room. Drake turned around.

"Come on, Toby! We have to go back. The man's home." But Toby didn't respond. He stood there staring unfocused down the hall. Drake wasn't even sure his friend had heard him.

"Toby, hurry up!" he pleaded, but Toby still didn't move. Instead he murmured, more to himself than to Drake, "I can make it. I have to."

"No, Toby! Don't!" Drake cried out, but his pleas were ignored. Toby sprinted down the long hallway toward the safety of the living room. He had almost made it past the door to the garage, when the man burst through.

CHAPTER 24

RAY FELT MUCH better. Amazing what a few drinks can do for your mood, he thought to himself. Well, maybe more than a few. But who's counting?

Ray turned down his street. The car swerved onto the other side of the road as he steered a wide arc into the driveway. The garage door slowly opened and he waved good-bye to Al who had followed him home after trying to convince him—to no avail—that he was in no condition to drive. Good old Al. What a pal, Ray thought, as his foot hit the accelerator pedal with more force than he intended. The car lurched forward into the gaping black opening of the garage and rammed into a metal wheelbarrow stored next to the back wall.

"Damn!" Ray swore. Unsteadily, he pushed himself out of the car.

✧   ✧   ✧

TOBY PANICKED. He had to get back to his corner. Drake had yelled something to him, but he couldn't hear the older dog's warning through the rush of fear roaring in his ears. He could make it. He knew he could. With his eyes riveted on the doorway to the living room, he ran as fast as he could.

Suddenly, the door leading to the garage flew open, blocking the hall and Toby's escape. He skidded to a halt a few inches from the implacable wooden barrier. He heard the man speaking directly above him on the other side of the door. The sound of his voice filled Toby with dread, and the terror that coursed through his body paralyzed him.

The door slammed shut.

The man hovered directly above him.

✦　✦　✦

"HEY HON, I'M HOME!" Lisa could smell the alcohol before he even opened his mouth. "How about a kiss hello?" he asked, and leaned forward. She turned her face and his kiss landed on her cheek.

"What's the matter? Can't I have a birthday kiss?"

Lisa turned away from him and entered the kitchen. "You can have a birthday kiss when you're sober again. For now, you need to go to sleep." He was pretty drunk. There wouldn't be any discussion tonight.

"I don't want to go to bed," he declared, and slammed the door shut behind him.

"I'm gonna watch some television."

Lisa knew arguing with him wouldn't do any good. He'd just end up passing out on the recliner anyway. She watched as he turned to head down the hallway to the family room. It was then that she noticed Toby standing in the middle of the hall directly in front of Ray. She started to warn her husband as he took a step forward, but it was too late. He tripped and fell over the dog.

"What the hell was that?" he yelled, as he sat up and rubbed his right elbow, which had taken the brunt of the fall. The walls of the hallway wavered back and forth as he tried to get his bearings. A white object came into focus on the floor directly in front of him. It was that stupid dog again!

"Damn dog!" he yelled out. "What the hell do you think you're doing?" Ray's anger erupted. The alcohol had worked to suppress his anger earlier, but now it only served to fuel his rage; a rage that now had a target—Toby.

Ray lashed his foot out at the dog. The toe of his shoe hit Toby's back leg.

"Ray! What are you doing? Stop it!"

Ray looked up. Lisa stood in the hall with a look of horror on her face. He clumsily pushed himself up from the floor and steadied himself with the support of the hallway walls.

"That damn dog tripped me! He needs to learn who's boss around here!" Ray looked down at where the dog had been standing, but the space was empty.

THE MAN STUMBLED over Toby and landed on the floor behind him. Toby felt the man's foot kick his leg. His right leg this time. The man began to yell. Toby felt the force of the rage emanating from him, a force he had experienced once before—one he did not want to experience ever again.

He turned and ran down the remainder of the hall into the living room. He had to reach his corner.

✧ ✧ ✧

"WHERE'D HE GO?" Ray yelled. Lisa didn't reply. "Where did that stupid dog go?"

Lisa stared at her husband, dumbstruck.

She found her voice.

"Leave him alone, Ray. He's only a puppy." Lisa tried to reason with her husband, but he was too drunk. He pushed past her and headed for the living room.

"I'm gonna get that dog once and for all! I should have finished him off the other night."

"Ray, don't," Lisa cried.

He burst into the living room.

Lisa was right behind him. He's crazed, she thought. How can I stop him?

✧ ✧ ✧

THE MAN ENTERED the living room, and the woman followed right behind him. Toby pushed himself deeper into the corner. He shut his eyes tightly as the man approached and prayed something or someone would stop the nightmare.

✧ ✧ ✧

HE WAS AT THE puppy's corner now, towering over the small, helpless form huddled under the end table. The room was still and only the sound of the clock ticking interrupted the silence that was indifferent to the violent storm raging inside Ray. He reached down to grab Toby. Lisa lunged at her husband to stop him just as a ferocious growl broke the silence.

✧ ✧ ✧

DRAKE DIDN'T hesitate; he leapt; teeth bared. He would not let the man hurt Toby again. His jaw clamped onto the man's left arm. His teeth easily pierced the fabric that covered it and sank deep into the muscle underneath.

✧ ✧ ✧

RAY SCREAMED and lashed at Drake, trying to break the dog's grip on his arm, but the dog held on.

"Get him off me!" he yelled; but Lisa could only watch, helplessly paralyzed by shock.

In desperation, Ray curled his right hand into a fist and slammed it into Drake's head connecting with a sickening crunch.

Lisa screamed.

He swung again.

Drake fell in a heap to the floor.

"What are you doing? Get away from Drake!" Justin ran down the stairs and pummeled his father with his fists. Jessica watched the terrifying scene from the staircase.

"The stupid animal attacked me!" Ray said, as he grabbed Justin's wrists and held him back. "He could have killed me! Look at my arm!"

His father was drunk.

Justin looked down at Drake lying still on the floor. The dog's eyes were open, but they had already begun to glaze over.

"You killed him! You killed Drake! How could you?" Justin yanked his wrists from his father's hold and fell to his knees next to still body of his dog.

"He attacked me! But you don't care, do you?" Ray lashed back. "You care more about that stupid mutt."

Justin stood up and faced his father.

"You hurt Marshmallow, didn't you? Did you try to hurt him again tonight? Is that why Drake attacked you?"

Ray raised his hand as if to slap his son. Justin backed up. "Why don't you pick on someone your own size? You're a coward! I hate you!"

Lisa grabbed Justin and pulled him out of the path of his father's rage.

Justin pulled free from his mother's grasp and picked up Toby from under the end table.

"I know you hurt Marshmallow, just like you hurt Drake. You hate the dogs and I hate you!" Justin turned and ran up the stairs with the puppy clutched to his chest, brushing past Jessica who still stood on the stairway in shock. Justin's bedroom door slammed shut. The room became quiet again, except for the ever-present ticking of the clock.

"You didn't really kill Drake, did you Daddy?" Jessica asked her father, unable to believe he was capable of such a thing.

Ray looked up at his daughter.

What had he done?

There was too much alcohol in his system for him to think clearly. He had to leave. Get away from the accusations, away from the look of trust and love on his daughter's face, and the look of disdain and disgust on his wife's. Without a word, he walked past Lisa and out of the living room.

✧ ✧ ✧

TOBY WATCHED IN horror as Drake fell limp to the floor. Was he okay? He had to be. Drake was his best friend—his only friend—and he had saved him from the man. But Toby knew better. He'd seen the face of death before.

The boy came running down the stairs. Yelling between the man and the boy ensued. Toby prayed it would stop as he frantically tried to block out what was happening. Suddenly, the boy grabbed him from his corner and ran up the stairs into his bedroom, slamming the door behind him. Once inside, the boy lay down on the bed tightly embracing Toby as he sobbed into his pillow.

Toby had to leave now. Drake was gone. There was nothing left for him here. He stared at the closed bedroom door that separated him from his freedom. It was a grim, implacable symbol of his physical and spiritual imprisonment.

Toby felt the tendrils of despair grab hold of him again. He fought back. His chance to escape would come.

The telltale noise of the man leaving rattled through the house. A short while later the boy's muffled crying subsided, replaced by the soft, rhythmic breathing of sleep. A few moments later he heard a gentle rapping on the bedroom door. A stream of light from the hallway escaped into the room as it slowly opened. The dark silhouette of the woman filled the opening. She moved toward the bed, bent over, and kissed the top of her son's head. She stood there for a moment, and then left as quietly as she had entered.

Darkness engulfed Toby again as the woman pulled the door shut. He closed his eyes to dwell in his inner darkness, but sleep eluded him. He opened his eyes and saw light seeping through the edge of the doorway. The woman had left the door open a crack!

Toby's eyes remained fixed on the thin band of light that represented his freedom. Without hesitation, he pulled himself out from under the boy's arm, which now lay loosely on top of him. The movement triggered the boy's reflexes, and he rolled over into the shadows. Toby jumped off the bed and ran to the door. He pushed the door open wider with his paw and silently moved to the top of the stairs.

Muted sounds came from the family room below. The living room light was on, beckoning him down. Toby started down the steps, and then stopped. Would Drake's body still be lying there? Toby forced himself to descend the remaining stairs.

A blanket lay over Drake; Drake's blanket. The one he always slept on.

Tears welled in his eyes, but there was no time to grieve the loss of his friend. He had to keep moving. There would be time enough for grieving later.

"Good-bye, Drake. I'll never forget you," Toby whispered, as he snuck through the living room and into the kitchen. He pushed through the rubber flap of the cat door and stepped out into the foggy night.

CHAPTER 25

SINCE HIS HEART attack two years earlier, Mr. Olsen had walked the one mile distance around the block of his neighborhood every night. He preferred walking at night; it was quiet and peaceful then.

He opened the front door and pulled his coat off the hook. The night was chilly and a dense fog shrouded the world.

✧ ✧ ✧

A THICK GRAY MIST surrounded Toby. Trepidation grew in him as he realized his plan for escape did not extend beyond the deck where he stood. Behind him, he heard the soft sound of the rubber flap. He turned. Meesha stood before him with a look of surprise on her face. Behind her, Pinka stepped through the flap and bumped into her sister's back end.

"What are you doing out here?" Meesha demanded, and then continued before Toby could reply. "Who let you out?

You're not supposed to be out here by yourself at night." Pinka moved next to her, and they both waited for his response.

"I left the house the same way you did, through the flap."

Meesha, ignoring the defensive tone in his voice, gave him the most incredulous look she could muster. "You're not supposed to use our door. It's for cats only."

"Oh, yeah? Well, this isn't the first time I've used it, but it will be the last."

"Why will it be the last?" Pinka asked, finally able to get a word in.

"Because I'm leaving," Toby announced.

Meesha and Pinka looked at each other. Meesha spoke first. "Where are you going?"

"I'm not sure yet; anywhere but here."

"Why are you leaving?" Pinka asked.

Toby looked down at the wooden deck. "I'm running away."

"Running away?" Meesha asked. "Running away from what?"

"The man," Toby replied.

"Oh," replied Meesha with a knowing look on her face. Toby was glad she didn't probe him for more details.

"You'll need our help to get out of the neighborhood. Pinka and I can guide you part of the way, but once we reach the outskirts, you're on your own."

"I'd appreciate any help you can give me." Toby was grateful for their willingness to help him. Maybe he'd miss them a little bit, too. "Are there any farms nearby?"

Pinka answered. "One of the other cats in the neighborhood used to live on a farm, but I don't know where."

"We'd better get started," Meesha said. "It's going to start raining soon and I, for one, do not like to get wet." She took the lead. Toby and Pinka followed her down the steps and onto a brick path that led to the side of the house. Meesha turned left and took them along a tall hedgerow toward the back of the yard. She stopped and looked back at her followers.

"We're going to stick to the backyards as much as possible. A couple of houses down, though, we'll have to take a detour. Thor lives there. He isn't very friendly, at least not to cats, though I don't know why anyone wouldn't like cats." Meesha paused as if she were actually considering her statement. "Anyway, we'll use the walkway along the street to circumvent his yard. After that we're home free until we reach the main road. That's where we'll have to part."

Meesha turned and disappeared through a small break in the hedge, which created an opening just large enough for them to go single file into the next yard.

Toby started through the dark passageway; wet hemlock branches brushed against his fur. Several seconds later he came out on the other side of the bushes where Meesha stood impatiently waiting for them. A moment later Pinka emerged behind Toby. Without a word Meesha turned and continued across the wet grass. Patches of mist thinned and thickened as they progressed and a fine drizzle of rain began to fall.

There was no barrier between the yard they were in and the next yard, but as they silently moved on, a tall wooden fence materialized out of the fog barring their passage.

"That's where Thor lives," Meesha informed Toby.

"We're going to cut down to the street here. Hopefully, he won't detect us. His bark is very loud." Meesha led Toby and Pinka along the side of the house that occupied the lot. The building was dark and looming in the foggy night. The group passed cautiously through the dark cloak of its shadow as they made their way to the street.

Loud barking suddenly broke the silence.

"Quick!" Meesha said. "Back this way!"

Toby and Pinka, startled by the barking, hastened after her. Meesha ran back the way they had come and disappeared into two bushes growing next to the side of the building. Toby poked his head into the retreat.

"Hurry up!" Meesha urged him. "Where's Pinka?"

"I'm right here," her sister replied, as she entered the small cavity behind Toby. Though there wasn't much space, the three fit comfortably beneath the interlaced branches of the two bushes. A few water droplets found their way through the thick layers of the dense foliage, but were quickly absorbed once they hit the ground.

"That was Thor," said Meesha.

"I figured as much," said Toby. "He sounds ferocious."

"Oh, he is," Pinka assured him. "He's twice as big as Drake and he's all black. You can't even see him at night." A memory stirred in Toby as Pinka spoke; the memory of another large, black, ferocious dog. The dog that had killed his sister what seemed like a lifetime ago.

"He can't escape, can he?" Toby asked.

"He escaped once when the gate was left open. He just about terrorized everyone in the neighborhood that day. Remember, Pinka?"

"I certainly do. He caused a huge ruckus around here."

Toby knew if he didn't stop them the two sisters would embark on a lengthy recollection of the incident, and Toby didn't have time for that. "So what are we going to do now?" he asked Meesha.

"We'll approach the street from this side of the house. I should have taken us this way in the first place."

The sound of raindrops hitting the outer layer of the bush became louder.

"We'd better leave now before the rain gets worse," Meesha announced. "Stay close."

One by one the three left the comfort of the small hideaway. Meesha led the way down to the road. Once there, they continued up the sidewalk that paralleled the street. Meesha peered ahead into the swirling gray mist as they proceeded.

She stopped.

A figure slowly emerged out of the fog on the path in front of them. Meesha and Pinka knew many of the humans in the neighborhood, but the figure was indistinguishable.

"Run!" Meesha yelled. She turned and fled. Pinka instantly reacted to her sister's warning and took off. Toby looked up and saw the large, dark shape approaching him.

"Toby, come on!" Meesha called out to him, but he didn't move.

✦ ✦ ✦

AS SOON AS MR. OLSEN stepped outside, the rain began to fall. He reached back and pulled the hood to his raincoat up over his head.

So deep were his musings as he walked that he almost

didn't see the small, white puppy in the middle of the sidewalk. Mr. Olsen recognized him right away. It was the Johnson dog. He had seen Lisa and Justin walking him on numerous occasions. What he was doing out on a night like this?

He half expected the puppy to turn and run as he approached, but the dog didn't move. Mr. Olsen leaned down, picked him up, and tucked him into his coat. The dog was drenched and shaking violently.

"I don't know what you're doing out here, little guy, but I'm going to take you home where you belong. Don't worry. Everything will be okay."

When Mr. Olsen reached the driveway of the Johnson house, he noticed a light on in the back room. He walked up the steps to the front door. Once on the landing, he paused. The doorbell glowed yellow-orange in the darkness, like a small beacon in the night. He reached out and pressed the button.

Thankfully, after the horrible scene with Drake, Ray had left the house. Lisa couldn't face him after what had happened. After she settled Jessica into bed and checked in on Justin, she sat in the family room and tried to clear her mind. The puppy had to leave the house; there was no doubt of that. She was frightened for his life. She could never live with herself if something happened to the dog. Justin would be heartbroken, but the alternative was worse.

Tracy, she had to call Tracy. She would take Marshmallow.

The doorbell pealed throughout the house, jolting Lisa from her thoughts.

"Who could that be?" she wondered aloud, and jumped out of the recliner and hurried to the front door. Had something happened to Ray? When she reached the door, she switched on the outside light and peered through the peephole. Mr. Olsen stood outside! What was he doing here at this time of night?

Lisa quickly unlocked the door and pulled it open.

"Good evening, Mrs. Johnson. Sorry to bother you so late, but I came across this little guy while I was taking my nightly walk."

Lisa's jaw dropped when she saw Toby's water-drenched head sticking out from under the protective cover of Mr. Olsen's coat. The dog was trembling.

"I'm sorry, come in, Mr. Olsen," Lisa said, recovering from her initial surprise. She stepped back, allowing room for him to enter the foyer. Thankfully, he couldn't see Drake's covered body in the living room from where he stood.

"What's going on, Ma? Who's here?" Justin, awakened by the sound of the doorbell, stood in his pajamas at the top of the stairs.

"Mr. Olsen, our neighbor. He has Marshmallow. He found him outside while he was taking his walk."

"Marshmallow!" Justin raced down the steps.

Mr. Olsen carefully took Toby out from under his coat.

"Marshmallow, what happened? How did you get outside?" Justin asked, as he took the shivering, wet puppy in his arms. "Where did you find him?"

"On the sidewalk in front of the Tuckers' house," Mr. Olsen replied. "He was just standing there on the sidewalk in the rain. I saw your cats run off when I approached, but this little guy didn't move so I scooped him up."

Justin turned to his mother. "How did he get out? He was in my room with me and the door was shut."

"I don't know," Lisa said, just as puzzled as her son. "I didn't let him out." How did the dog get out? Just then she heard the cats enter the house through the rubber flap in the kitchen door. Meesha and Pinka walked into the room. They looked like a couple of drowned rats.

Suddenly, the answer hit her. The cat door! The puppy was still small enough to fit through the opening.

"The cat door," she said aloud.

"What?" Justin asked, puzzled.

"He must have left the house through the cat door. It's the only explanation. He's small enough to fit through the opening. I must have left your bedroom door open when I went upstairs to check on you."

"Makes sense," said Mr. Olsen. "He probably decided to go out and do some exploring with the cats."

Justin looked down at Toby and gently chastised him. "You could've gotten lost, Marshmallow; don't ever do that again!"

"Thank goodness you happened to be outside walking, Mr. Olsen. Otherwise, who knows what might have happened? You saved his life!"

"I didn't really do anything. You probably should thank the rain. I usually walk the other direction around the block, but the rain would have been driving at me tonight."

"Well, thank you anyway. We appreciate what you did."

"I'm going to get going now and let you tend to your puppy," Mr. Olsen said, and turned to leave. "I just hope the little guy is okay and doesn't catch a cold or become sick." He pulled his hood back over his head.

"We'll dry him off and put him right to bed," said Lisa. "Thanks again, Mr. Olsen."

"Yeah, Mr. Olsen, thanks a lot," Justin repeated.

"No problem. You take care of yourselves now." Mr. Olsen stepped out onto the small porch and closed the door behind him.

CHAPTER 26

IT WAS A NIGHTMARE!

Toby couldn't believe it. He was back in the house again! A howl of frustration grew within him, but it was checked by the incessant shuddering of his cold, damp body. For the time being, he gave in to defeat and to the heavy weariness that descended upon him.

A voice came from far away.

"Toby," it called to him sweetly.

The darkness that had blanketed his sleep became illuminated by a white radiance that emanated from all directions. The light enveloped Toby and vanquished the darkness.

"Toby," the voice came again, this time clearer, and closer than before. A familiar voice. Toby raised his head. A white figure glided toward him.

Tara!

Toby jumped up and ran to her; his fatigue vanished.

"Tara, is it really you?"

"Yes, Toby."

"I'm so happy to see you. I've missed you so much. You don't know how much."

"I know, Toby. I've missed you, too."

Toby looked around. "Where are we? How did I . . . how did we get here?"

"You're dreaming, Toby. This is the only way I can communicate with you."

Toby looked puzzled. "This is a dream? But everything seems so real."

"Dreams are just another form of reality, Toby."

"Are you alive?" he asked.

Tara thought for a moment. She wanted to give him an answer that made sense in his world. "In a way; I exist in a world that is very different from the old world, from your world. I don't have a physical body, even though you can see me. It's more . . . a spiritual body," she said. The answer seemed to satisfy Toby for now.

"Can you stay with me?" Toby asked. "I don't want you to leave again."

"No, I can't stay. But someday, when your time comes, we will be together again, forever. For now, I can visit you in your dreams."

Toby was confused by his sister's words. The scared, vulnerable Tara he knew was gone. This Tara was older, wiser, and more confident. His sister continued.

"I know you are going through a difficult time right now and you think running away is the answer to your problem, but try to have faith that the humans will do what is best for you. The woman is a good person. In the end she

will protect you and keep you from harm. Trust me if you cannot trust the humans."

The figure that embodied Tara's spirit began to fade, slowly dissolving into the light. "I must leave now. I can only stay for a short time when I visit. But I will come to you again."

"Where are you going, Tara?"

The vision was almost gone.

"Come back!" Toby cried out.

The voice came again from far away.

"Remember what I said Toby and have faith." The apparition vanished and darkness descended until the light was extinguished.

"MA, HOW ARE WE going to keep Marshmallow from going outside again?" Justin asked, after placing a small towel on top of Toby's damp, shivering body.

Lisa sat on the couch in the family room. She beckoned Justin to sit down next to her and took a deep breath.

"Justin, I know how much you love Marshmallow, but after what happened tonight . . ." she hesitated. "He can't stay here, honey. He just can't. We have to protect him. It's our responsibility to do that."

Her son remained silent.

"I'm going to ask Tracy to take him, at least for now." Lisa stopped and waited for a response from her son. There was none immediately, but when one came, it came with full force.

"I hate Dad for this!" Justin yelled. "I hate him more

than anything in the whole world! He killed Drake, and now he's making you take Marshmallow from me!" He stood up and ran out of the room.

"Justin!" Lisa called out after him. She wanted to console her son, ease his pain, but he was already up the stairs. She heard his bedroom door slam shut for the second time that night.

Lisa forced herself up from the couch and went over to where the puppy lay. A shiver coursed through his body as she rubbed the towel against his fur. Poor thing, she thought. He's been through so much. At least at Tracy's, he'd be safe. She went to the end table and picked up the telephone.

The rain quickly covered Tracy's glasses with large drops as she ran from the car to the front door of her house. She could feel water begin to seep through her shoes as she fumbled in her pocketbook for the keys. Once inside the house, she switched on the inside hall light and turned to shut the door. One of the cats darted inside.

Tracy found herself boxed in by two of her three dogs, both waiting for their ritual greeting. The oldest dog had a bad case of arthritis in his hips and rarely got up to greet her anymore.

She patted the two younger dogs on the head and went into the kitchen to check her answering machine; one message. Could it be Jeff, the guy she had just met at the club? She pressed the play button.

"Tracy, this is Lisa. Please call me as soon as you get in. I don't care what time it is. It's important. I need your help." Tracy quickly picked up the handset and dialed Lisa's number. She hoped everything was okay. Since Ray had started drinking again, Tracy's stomach turned every time Lisa called or left a message.

Lisa grabbed the telephone.

"Hello?"

"Lisa, its Tracy. What's wrong?"

"Oh, Tracy, Drake is dead. Ray killed him. I need you to take Marshmallow before he ends up killing him, too."

Tracy only hesitated for a moment to let her friend's words sink in.

"I'll be right over. I'm leaving now."

Tracy pulled into the driveway and shut off the car. She ran up the steps to the front door where Lisa stood waiting and wrapped her arms around her best friend. Lisa began to sob.

"My God, Lisa, what happened?"

Lisa tried to compose herself. She didn't want to wake the kids.

"Drake's body is still in the living room. I covered him with his blanket . . . he's too heavy for me to move." She wiped tears from her face with the back of her hand.

"Don't worry, Lisa. I'll help you move Drake." Tracy still could not believe the words she was hearing.

"No, you have to take Marshmallow and leave. If Ray comes home and the dog is still here . . ."

"Okay," Tracy said. "Whatever you want; I'll take the

puppy and leave. We'll talk tomorrow. I'll call you from work. But if you need me, call me. I don't care what time it is. Okay?"

Lisa nodded.

"He's in the pet carrier ready to go. You can keep it for him. He fits in it perfectly." Her voice broke, but she continued. "I put all of the dog food we had into a bag for you to take since we won't need it." Her voice cracked again. "Now leave, quickly, before Ray comes home."

Lisa stood at the door and watched her friend pull out of the driveway. Tears rolled down her cheeks. She continued to stand there after the car was out of sight and wondered if Justin would ever forgive her.

PART V
A New Home
For Toby

✧　✧　✧

"We call them dumb animals,
and so they are
for they cannot tell us how they feel,
but they do not suffer less
because they have no words."

— Anna Sewell, Black Beauty, 1877

CHAPTER 27

TRACY DROVE PAST the large blue and white sign in front of the old brick building of the Humane Society and pulled into the employee parking lot. She took the first open spot.

Once inside her office, Tracy placed the carrier on the floor. She bent down and cooed to the puppy inside as she opened the cage door and carefully took him out. She softly kissed him on the top of his head and held his trembling body against hers as she carried him down the hall to the section of the building that housed the dogs up for adoption. The puppies were kept in a separate pen from the older dogs. There were currently five puppies up for adoption, all four months or younger in age. At six months, Toby would be the oldest.

The barking of dogs, which up to now had been muted, fully accosted her when she opened the door to the kennel area. The puppy's pen was at the end of a wide corridor that separated two rows of cages lining each side of the large room. The puppies began to bark as Tracy approached their cage. She unlatched the door and slipped into the pen, securing the door behind her. The raucous group bounded upon her, yelping and jumping up on her shins.

Tracy placed Toby on the floor. The curious puppies gathered around the newcomer who, after a moment, went to the back corner of the pen and lay down. The other puppies followed. Tracy noticed the fear in Toby's eyes begin to lessen as he began to interact with the other puppies. She wondered if it would ever go away completely. Tears welled up in her eyes. She blinked them back. The weekly staff meeting was in five minutes.

✧ ✧ ✧

TOBY WATCHED THE woman walk away. What is this place? he wondered. The pen he now found himself in with five other puppies was surrounded by similar pens all filled with dogs of various colors and sizes. Would the woman come back for him? Would she take him back home? He didn't want to go home. There was nothing left for him there but fear.

"What's your name?" an older black and white dog in the neighboring pen inquired.

"Toby."

"My name's Barkley. Welcome to the shelter. I was brought here last week. The people here are nice and the food's pretty good," he commented. "It beats living homeless on the streets."

"What's a shelter?" Toby asked.

"It's a place where homeless animals are brought," the older dog answered. "Mostly dogs, as you can see. There

are some cats in the other room and a couple of birds, or so I've been told."

"Oh," said Toby. "Does that mean I'm homeless now?"

"Probably," said Barkley. "Everyone I've met here so far has needed a home. Some of the animals have been here for a long time. Apparently they used to kill the dogs no one wanted to adopt, but now they stay here until someone wants them or another shelter takes them in."

Toby was stunned by the other dog's words. "They kill dogs here?"

"No. Not anymore. Though I did hear from one of the dogs I met that some places still put unwanted dogs 'to sleep'."

"To sleep?"

"To sleep permanently, if you know what I mean."

Toby thought he knew all too well what Barkley meant and the look of terror on his face bespoke his understanding.

"Oh, I didn't mean to scare you!" Barkley immediately responded to the younger dog's reaction. "You're safe here. Besides, most of the younger dogs, like you, get adopted right away. It's the older dogs, like me, who end up spending the longest time here."

Barkley's words relaxed Toby somewhat, and as the morning wore on the older dog's tales of his numerous adventures put Toby at further ease. This was the second shelter the older dog had been in since his original owner had died. The first family who adopted him had only kept him a short time.

"Apparently, I made too much noise," Barkley told Toby. "What did they expect? I'm a Beagle, and Beagles like to bark and howl. It's in our nature, you know."

"I didn't know," Toby replied. "What's a Beagle?"

"A Beagle is a breed of dog. That's why we all look different. We come from different families of dogs. Each family or breed has different traits and characteristics."

"I see," said Toby, though he didn't understand completely. The older dog was very knowledgeable and experienced. In some ways he reminded Toby of Drake, which made Toby happy and sad at the same time.

"You're very unusual looking," Barkley commented. "What breed are you?"

Toby paused for a moment. He had never been asked that question before.

"I don't know," he replied, "but my Mama told me my grandfather was a white wolf."

"A white wolf, huh? That explains the color of your fur," Barkley said. "I've never met a wolf, so I don't know what they look like, but you look a lot like a German Shepherd I used to know. Anyway, it doesn't matter. We're all the same inside!"

"We are?"

"Sure we are," Barkley declared. "We all need to eat and sleep and like to have our tummies scratched. We need companionship and love—most of us anyway. I have met dogs that would rather be alone. To each their own, I say. Maybe something bad happened to them to make them want to be isolated from others."

"I never thought about it that way," Toby replied, awed by the wisdom in the other dog's words.

"You would have come to the same conclusion yourself, I'm sure," said Barkley. "Don't forget, I'm much older than you and I've had plenty of time to think about my experiences and observations, especially during my stays in shelters."

Toby thought for a moment. "Maybe I'll become wise like you if I stay in the shelter long enough," he said.

"Don't wish for that, Toby," Barkley said more harshly than he intended. He softened his voice and continued. "Shelter life is lonely. You make a friend one day and the next day they're gone." Barkley looked down for a moment, averting Toby's gaze. When he looked back up, his eyes were moist. "You're young. Your whole life is ahead of you. Don't wish for loneliness; it comes too easily and stays too long."

The older dog turned from the wiring separating the two cages and lay down next to his water bowl. "I'm tired, Toby. I need to rest. We'll talk again later, okay?" Without waiting for an answer, Barkley laid his head on his paws and closed his eyes.

During the course of the day many humans came into the large room and walked up and down the aisles looking at the dogs. Almost all of them spent time at the puppy's pen. Whenever people approached, Toby curled up in the corner and kept to himself. One of them reminded him of the man back home. A shiver coursed through Toby's body at the sight of him.

At the end of the day, after the woman finished putting food and fresh water in all the pens, she walked over to the cage with the pet carrier.

"Looks like you're leaving," Barkley commented. "Maybe you're not homeless after all."

"Maybe," Toby said with uncertainty. The fear of being

taken back to the man's house pierced through the tenuous peace of mind he had slowly attained as the day wore on.

"Well, good luck to you, Toby."

"You too, Barkley, I hope you find a home where you're not lonely anymore and you can make as much noise as you want."

"Me, too," said the older dog, as he watched yet another new friend leave his life. "Me, too."

✧ ✧ ✧

TRACY PICKED UP the carrier and turned off the light in her office. As she walked down the hall, she marveled at all the people who had asked her about the 'beautiful white puppy' that day. She had never seen so much curiosity about one of the dogs.

Almost everyone who came into the kennel had questioned her about him, and each time she had given the same answer. "He's not up for adoption; I'm just watching him for a friend." And each time, a thin veil of disappointment would fall over the inquirer's face as he or she reluctantly moved on to the next pen.

CHAPTER 28

"MA, CAN WE STOP at the Humane Society to see the animals on the way home?" Matt asked, as he leaned against the back of the front passenger seat.

His mother turned. "What are you doing out of your seatbelt?"

"My seatbelt is on. I just loosened it a little."

"Well, tighten it back up, mister." Holly reached up and tilted the rearview mirror so it captured the partial image of the twelve-year-old sitting behind her.

Matt looked up from readjusting the strap and caught his mother looking at him.

"Did you tighten it snugly?" she asked.

"Yes, but you didn't answer my question," Matt replied. "Can we stop at the Humane Society? Please?"

"Okay, okay," Holly relented. She repositioned the mirror and sighed. Matt would see at least one cat or dog he'd want to take home, some poor orphaned creature with big sad eyes; and she was just as bad as he was in that regard. She summoned her resolve to leave the Humane

Society without any new family members. They already had a cat and two goldfish. The small four-room house they rented was full enough.

"There's the road!" Matt exclaimed suddenly.

Holly flicked on the turn signal and pulled off the turnpike.

"Don't forget that we're just looking, okay?" Holly reminded him.

"I know, Ma. Don't worry," he assured her.

Tracy poured the remaining dog food into the last bowl, and then checked her wristwatch. Only a half an hour until closing time. The day had seemed especially long. Saturdays were always the busiest. Most people who stopped in on the weekends did so as a second thought while they were out shopping or visiting friends and came in just to look. Some of the visitors came with the intention of adopting, but not nearly enough.

No one was visiting now, so when the door to the kennel area slammed shut, the sound startled her. That door needs to be fixed, she thought. The loud noise scared some of the older, more nervous dogs. She could see why.

A woman and a young boy had entered the room. Tracy had seen them at the kennel before.

She picked up the bowl of food and carried it over to the cage next to Toby's. The old Beagle got up from the corner as she approached. His tail wagged as he waited in anticipation for his supper. She opened the door and set the bowl down.

Tracy moved over to the puppy's pen. Three weeks had

passed since she had picked Toby up from Lisa's and the interest in him from people looking to adopt a dog had not diminished. She spoke with Lisa on the telephone daily. Her friend appeared to be losing her initial resolve to keep the dog out of the house. And though Ray was going to AA again, Tracy would not stand mutely by and let Lisa take the dog back to live in the house where he had experienced so much terror. Not while Ray inhabited it.

Holly slowly walked along the cage fronts, stopping to look at each dog as she moved down the aisle. All of the enclosures were occupied and some had more than one dog in them. Matt had moved up the aisle several cages ahead of her. A woman with a denim apron and bright red hair tied back in a pony tail walked up the aisle past Matt toward Holly. The woman smiled and said hello as she approached.

"Are you interested in adopting a dog?" she asked Holly.

"Oh, no, we just stopped by on the way home from shopping to look at the animals. My son loves seeing the dogs."

"Do you have any dogs?"

"No, we have a cat," Holly replied.

"I have three cats, three dogs and two birds. As you can imagine, my house is a zoo; literally."

Holly laughed, and then asked, "Do the cats and dogs get along?"

"Oh, sure, they get along fine. It's always hard when a new animal comes into the house. Most animals are territorial, but after a week or two things usually work out."

"Ma, you've got to come see this dog! He's so cool! He's all white!" Matt excitedly called out to his mother

"Okay, just a minute. I'll be right there," Holly said, and turned back to Tracy.

"He must be talking about Marshmallow," said Tracy. "He belongs to a friend of mine." Holly followed Tracy to Toby's cage. At first Holly didn't see him. Her attention was drawn to the Beagle eating in a pen next to where Matt was kneeling on the floor. She shifted her line of sight and spotted the white dog lying in the back corner of the enclosure. She gasped. He was the most beautiful dog she had ever seen. His fur was pure white except for the touches of buff that dusted the tips of his ears and tail. His chestnut brown eyes peered out of the soft whiteness of his face.

Holly looked into his eyes. The sadness emanating from them pierced her heart. She held her breath for a moment.

Tracy interrupted Holly from her thoughts. "This is Marshmallow. As I said, I'm watching him for a friend of mine."

With a solemn look on her face, Holly turned to Tracy and asked quietly, "What happened to him?"

She considered Holly for a moment. The woman appeared to be greatly affected by the dog, and Toby's story began to involuntarily spill from Tracy's mouth. She told Holly all she knew about his past.

Holly was riveted to Tracy's every word. Tears pooled in the corners of her eyes and unashamedly fell down her cheeks.

"Would you like a tissue?" Tracy asked, and without waiting for an answer, she pulled one from her apron pocket and handed it to Holly.

"Are you okay, Ma?" Matt asked.

Holly sniffed. "I'm fine, honey. That's such a sad story. How could anyone hurt a defenseless puppy?" She looked back at the dog still crouched in the corner, and tears began to well up again.

"I probably shouldn't have told you what happened to him," Tracy said. "Almost everyone who came in today asked me about him, but you're the first person I felt compelled to tell his tale. I don't know why. I guess I sensed something different about you; your compassion."

"I'll take that as a compliment," Holly said with a partial smile, as she dabbed the tissue on her face. "Though sometimes it's a curse."

"I know what you mean," Tracy said.

Holly beckoned Tracy several feet down the aisle away from where Matt still sat on his knees in front of Toby's cage. "When will you know whether your friend wants to take him back or not?" Holly asked.

"I'm not sure. I've been pushing her for a decision, but . . ." Tracy shrugged her shoulders.

"Would you call me if she decides not to take him back?"

Tracy cocked her head at Holly. "Are you interested in adopting him?"

Holly hesitated, and then said, "This might sound weird, but I feel a connection with that dog. Almost like a feeling of déjà vu. I can't explain it."

Tracy hesitated. If the woman really was serious about

adopting the dog, she owed it to her to tell her the rest of his story; the one part she had left out. Tracy glanced over at Matt still kneeling on the floor.

"There's something else I need to tell you about Marshmallow," Tracy said, and lowered her voice. "The vet who examined him and his sister in California thought the pups might be part wolf."

"Part wolf?" Holly asked in surprise. "What made him think that?"

"He worked with wolf-dog hybrids in Minnesota a number of years ago and seemed to think Marshmallow and his sister might have some wolf blood in them. He did reassure my friend, though, that it was probably only a small amount, if any, and that she shouldn't be worried about it. I just thought you should know everything about him before you decide whether or not you want to adopt him; assuming my friend agrees to give him up."

Holly glanced over at Toby's pen then back at Tracy.

"Has he shown any signs of being vicious at all?"

Tracy laughed, and then caught herself. "I'm sorry, but Marshmallow is the least vicious dog I've ever encountered."

"Then I don't care," Holly said. "That dog is meant to be with me. I can feel it. He needs me."

"Are you sure?"

"Yes, absolutely."

"Okay. Give me your telephone number, and I'll call my friend tonight," Tracy said, as she pulled a pen and small piece of rumpled paper out of her apron pocket and handed them to Holly. "I can't promise anything."

"I know, but will you call me either way?" asked Holly,

as she wrote the information down and handed the pen and paper back to Tracy.

"Of course," said Tracy.

"I'm not going to mention this to my son. He's always wanted a dog and I don't want to get his hopes up."

"I understand," said Tracy.

Tracy walked Holly and her son to the main entrance and locked the door behind them. I'd better call Lisa tonight and push her for an answer, she thought. I may have just found a new home for Marshmallow.

CHAPTER 29

HOLLY LAY IN BED staring at the dimly lit ceiling. The dog she had seen at the kennel haunted her. She couldn't get him out of her mind. His brown, sorrowful eyes stared back at her wherever she looked. Questions whizzed through her mind. Would Tracy's friend decide to give him up for adoption? And if she did, did Holly really want a dog, especially a dog with such special needs? Holly pushed the negative thoughts from her mind and focused on the details Tracy had told her about the dog's past; a past that began in a box next to a dumpster on the other side of the country. Who had left him and his sister there, and why? Was he really part wolf? If so, how had that happened? Shifting her position several more times, she finally fell asleep, no closer to the answers than she was before.

The shrill ringing of the alarm clock awakened her. Holly reached over, pressed the snooze button, and lay back down. Then she remembered the dog she had seen at the kennel. A queer feeling filled her stomach. What had she been thinking? She didn't know the first thing about dogs. When she was a child, some of her friends had dogs. They were fun to play with, but she had never owned a dog, and had never wanted to.

Until now.

There was something different about this dog. She felt an attachment to him, a link, as if he were a kindred spirit. The previous night she had gone next door to see her landlord, Mrs. Sullivan, to ask if it would be okay if they got a dog. Mrs. Sullivan thought it was a great idea; it would give her dog Bailey a friend to play with. The alarm rang again. Holly rolled over, hit the off button, and threw off the bedcovers. The room was chilled from the cold November air that had seeped in through the window she always left cracked open at night. She pushed down the sash and got ready for work.

Tracy stood in the lobby of the restaurant waiting for Lisa. She needed to press her friend for a decision. Marshmallow needed a stable home.

Tracy glanced at her watch again and looked back through the lobby's large glass window just in time to see Lisa's car pull into a parking space in front of the restaurant.

After the waitress took their order, Tracy leaned forward in her chair and got right to the point. "So, have you made up your mind about Marshmallow?" Lisa looked down at her hands on her lap. After a few seconds, she looked up again. "I'm not sure what to do, Tracy. I'm torn." Tears filled her eyes.

"I know how much you loved Drake," said Tracy. "And I'm so sorry for what happened. But that's why I know you'll make the right decision for Marshmallow. He needs a safe, secure home, and I can't keep him indefinitely." Tracy let her words sink in for a moment before she continued. "He's been traumatized and needs a lot of love and attention."

"Okay. Okay, I hear you," Lisa said. She paused, and then relented. "Call the woman you told me about and tell her she can have him."

Tracy sat back in her chair, took a deep breath, and focused on her friend. "You're doing the right thing, you know."

"I know," said Lisa. "It's just hard because of Justin. He's so upset by all this."

"I realize this is going to be difficult for Justin, but Marshmallow can't stay in your house with Ray there," Tracy said. "I'll call Holly as soon as I get back to the office. You'd like her, Lisa. She has a good heart."

The waitress arrived with their meals and placed the plates in front of them. Tracy began to eat; she was glad the hard part of the lunch was out of the way.

The office cafeteria was crowded and noisy. Holly scanned the tables. She had spoken briefly with Tracy earlier that morning and hoped to hear back on her friend's decision soon. In the meantime, she had asked John, a co-worker, to meet her for lunch. He had more experience with dogs than anyone else she knew, and she wanted his advice.

Holly threaded her way through the closely packed tables and spotted John sitting next to the window.

"This place is a zoo!" she exclaimed, as she set her tray on the table and dropped into the chair.

"So, you're thinking of getting a dog, huh?" John asked.

Holly had told him a little about the dog, but she hadn't told him about the abuse yet, or about the fact that he might be part wolf. She had decided to keep the latter detail to herself.

"I'm thinking about it. That's why I wanted to talk to you. You seem to know a lot about dogs, and this one is kind of . . . special."

John suspended his roast beef sandwich in midair and gave Holly a puzzled look. "What do you mean by 'special'?"

"Matt and I saw him at the humane society this past Saturday. Tracy, the woman who's watching him now, said he's seven months old." Holly paused.

"So what makes him 'special'?" John asked.

Holly hesitated, and then said, "He was physically abused."

"How bad?"

"Pretty bad. He's afraid to move when people are around and he barely walks at all. Tracy has to carry him from place to place."

John put down his sandwich. "What happened to him?"

Holly proceeded to tell John what Tracy had told her about Toby. As she told the story, John became visibly upset, and at the end, he shook his head and said, "What kind of person would do something like that? Why get a dog if you don't want one? People who abuse animals should be locked in jail and the key thrown away." He picked up his sandwich and angrily bit into the roll. While chewing his food, he asked, "What kind of dog is he?"

"He's a German Shepherd mix. All white."

"All white, huh? That's unusual. You don't see too many white German Shepherd dogs."

"Do you think I'd be crazy to adopt a dog that's been abused?"

John put his sandwich down and leaned back in his chair. "I don't know about it being crazy, but it'll take a lot of patience and work to gain his trust and get him to open up to you. It can be done, but he may never get over it completely."

Holly sat in silence.

"You've already made up your mind, haven't you?" John asked.

"I know it sounds corny, but I have some kind of connection with this dog that I can't explain. He needs me."

John observed Holly for a few moments, and then said, "I know an excellent dog trainer who could give you some advice. She's great at working with dogs with special needs. I'll call you with her number when I get back to my office."

"Thanks, John. I really appreciate it," Holly said, as they got up from the table.

John was right, Holly thought, as she rode the elevator up to her office. Her mind had been made up the moment she had looked into Toby's eyes.

"There you are!" Holly's secretary Lynne said, as Holly passed by. "You just had a call not more than a minute ago. Someone named Tracy. She didn't say where she was calling from, but she left a number where you can reach her."

Holly's heart skipped a beat at the mention of Tracy's name. "Thanks, Lynne," she said, and closed her office door behind her. She sat down at her desk, grabbed the telephone handset, and quickly punched in the number.

The seconds ticked by while Holly waited for Tracy to pick up. What if it's bad news? She anguished. What if Tracy's friend wants to keep the dog?

"This is Tracy. May I help you?"

"Tracy, its Holly Baker. I just received the message that you called."

"Hi, Holly. That was quick."

Holly couldn't stand the suspense. "Did your friend make a decision yet?"

"As a matter of fact, I had lunch with her today, and she's decided to let you take Marshmallow."

Holly couldn't contain herself. "Oh, that's wonderful! I'm so happy, and Matt will be thrilled. How soon can I pick him up?"

"As soon as you want. I'll be here until six or so tonight if you want to pick him up after work."

Holly didn't hesitate. "I'll leave work around four, pick up Matt from the after-school program, and then we can go to the pet store. What do I need to buy for Marshmallow?"

"Just some puppy food and a leash and collar," Tracy suggested. "And you should probably buy him a small bed to sleep in. Dogs like having a place of their own to sleep."

"Okay. I'll see you around five-thirty."

"Sounds good," said Tracy.

Holly placed the handset back in its cradle. The doubts that had nagged her were gone, replaced by elation and joy.

CHAPTER 30

BARKLEY HAD BEEN surprised to see Toby again. But after several days of the woman taking the small white dog home and bringing him back to the kennel each morning, he told Toby that was a sign she was going to keep him. All of the other dogs that needed homes remained at the kennel each night.

Being an older dog, Barkley slept much of the day. All but one of the puppies had been adopted, so Toby spent much of his time sleeping, too. His dreams provided him temporary relief from the uncertainty that still shadowed his waking hours. And now, with Barkley and the remaining puppy soundly sleeping once again, Toby closed his eyes. The cacophony of kennel sounds soon blended together and became a soothing hum that lulled him to sleep.

A cool breeze carrying the scents of late fall gently blew across Toby's face. The sun's rays periodically won the battle with the passing clouds and their warmth caressed *his body. The notion that there shouldn't be a breeze in the kennel didn't occur to Toby immediately, but when it did, his confusion transformed into amazement as he looked about him. Several feet away, Drake slept peacefully on the grass next to the old oak tree where the boy sat sideways on the swing pushing back and forth with one foot. To Toby's left, the house sat just where he expected it to be, solid and implacable. And through the kitchen window, he could see the woman as she moved back and forth inside.*

Had the past few weeks all been a bad dream; a nightmare played out in his sleep? The experience couldn't have been a dream . . . yet everything around him seemed so real.

Toby tried to get up to run to Drake, but he found he could not move. His heart started racing. Everything around him began to spin. Vertigo threatened to swallow him. Toby closed his eyes to ward off the sickening sensation.

"Toby, are you all right?"

His eyelids slowly opened to the familiar voice and found Drake standing before him.

"Drake! You're alive!" Toby tried to sit up, but his body felt too heavy.

"Don't try to move, Toby. Just rest. You need your strength."

"But I'm home now! I want to get up and run and play with you and the boy."

Drake looked down. The solemn look on his face contradicted Toby's joy. He spoke quietly. "This is a dream, Toby."

Toby stared at his friend in bewilderment.

"But, Drake . . ."

His friend quieted him by raising his paw.

"Don't you remember? The man . . . what happened when I tried to protect you from him?"

Toby tried to find his voice. The memory of Tara visiting him in his dream came back to him.

Drake looked deep into Toby's eyes.

Toby shook his head in denial. Was it true? Could the dead really visit you in your dreams? Vertigo returned. He closed his eyes.

"It's okay, Toby. I'm happier where I am now. The pain in my leg is gone, and I feel young again. What happened was a blessing. But you, Toby, you have your whole life ahead of you. Make the most of the time you have. Learn to trust again. Learn to love again." Drake's voice began to fade. "Everything will work out in the end. You'll see. I'll visit you again soon."

Toby barely heard Drake's last words as the familiar scene around him faded.

Toby didn't know how much time had passed before he realized his face was cold and wet. He opened his eyes. A world of gray and white swirled around him. The ground on which he lay was covered with snow.

Was this another dream? Who would visit him in this dream?

As if in answer to his question, a large pack of wolves and dogs slowly materialized out of the enshrouding gray and one-by-one encircled him.

The snow stopped falling. All was still and quiet.

A long, wailing howl pierced the silence.

Followed by another.

Then another.

After a few moments, a chorus of howls erupted from the group that now surrounded Toby. A primordial urge rose within him. He stood up and shook off the light layer of snow that had accumulated on his fur. The urge grew stronger, more compelling, until he realized his own voice had joined the others. The multitude of voices became one as they howled on and on, until the cry reached its crescendo and abruptly ended, leaving an echoing silence around them once again.

A large, white figure approached Toby.

"Welcome to our pack, Toby." The figure turned, and with a nod of his head, indicated the others. He turned back to Toby. "How did you come to be here?"

Toby tried to find his voice, but the howl still reverberated in his throat. When he finally spoke, his reply was weak and raspy. "I don't know. I don't even know where here is." He hesitated, and then asked, "How do you know my name?"

"My name is Strider, Toby. I am your grandfather."

Strider! The memory of lying with Tara next to his mother as she told them the story of Sadie and Strider came flooding back to him and he felt a warmth of emotion flow through his body.

"Where is this place? How did I get here?" Toby asked.

Strider paused in thought for a moment, and then replied, "This land is a different place for different creatures, yet it is the same place for all creatures. For us," Strider swept his large head around him, "this is the place we call home."

Toby cocked his head and thought about his grandfather's explanation. "Can I stay here with you?" he asked. "Can this be my home, too?"

Strider considered his grandson.

"No, Toby. Not yet. Your time to join us will come to pass eventually, and when it does, we will be together forever. For now, you must go back to where you came from. You must find your home there."

"But I don't have a home there," said Toby.

"You will, Toby. I am sure of it. For now, come run with us. The experience will help ease the pain in your heart and soul."

Before Toby could reply, Strider turned and bounded off into the swirling snow that had begun to fall again. The others followed one by one. The same urge that had provoked Toby to howl earlier rose within him again, and he found himself running with the pack. They ran mile after mile in silent command of all around them. An exhilarating sense of freedom filled Toby. He stopped to howl for the pure joy of it, his nose stretched up toward the hidden sky. When the last note of his song died out, he lowered his head. The others were gone. He was alone.

As Toby began to wake up his senses belied his surroundings. He had just run through miles of snow, yet he felt warm and dry. His muscles should be tired and sore, but they felt strong and renewed; and the scents around him were not of a cold winter day, but of the kennel. He forced his eyes open. The now familiar view from inside his cage appeared before him.

"HOW MUCH LONGER before we're there?" Matt asked impatiently.

"We're almost there. Ten minutes or so," Holly replied, her excitement matching that of her son's.

Matt sat back in his seat and watched the scenery flash by the car window. He couldn't wait to get to the Humane Society. They were getting a dog! And not just any dog, a white dog!

"Matt," Holly said, "what do you think about changing Marshmallow's name? Marshmallow sounds kind of . . . I don't know . ."

"Would he care if we changed his name?" Matt asked. "Do you think it would confuse him?"

"I don't think so. He's still a puppy. He'd adjust to a new name pretty quickly."

"I don't really like the name Marshmallow either. It sounds kind of sissy for a boy dog," Matt said. "But his new name has to be one we both like, okay?"

"It's a deal," said Holly.

"What about Rocket?" he asked.

Rocket? she thought, and then said to her son, "Why don't we wait until we get to know him a little bit?"

"Okay," Matt said. "But let's not wait too long."

The sign for the Humane Society came up on the left.

"Here we are!" Holly announced. She felt nervous and excited at the same time.

"That was fast!" Matt said, ready to jump out of the car the moment it stopped.

Inside the kennel, Tracy leaned against the cage that housed Toby. He was in the same spot, in the same position, with the same scared look in his eyes. She wondered how he would fare at his new home. Would he ever completely recover from his trauma? Probably not, but hopefully he would recover enough to have a good life. She found herself missing him already.

The door to the kennel opened. Matt ran through, followed by Holly.

"Hi, there!" Tracy greeted them. "Marshmallow's all set to go!"

Matt ran over to the cage. "Hi, Marshmallow! We've come to take you home with us!" Matt turned and addressed Tracy. "My mother and I decided to give him a new name. Do you think that's okay?"

"To be honest with you, Matt, I'd change his name too if I were you."

"What would you name him?" he asked her.

"You and your mother need to decide that," she replied. "A name's a special thing. You'll know when you've found the right one."

Tracy turned to Holly. "I have some dog food you can take with you. He didn't eat much tonight, so you might want to give him some of the food when you get home."

"How much should we give him?" Holly asked.

"About a cup and a half should do it," Tracy answered. "And here's his pet carrier," she added, picking up the gray plastic carrier on the floor next to the cage. "I'll put him in here and help you out to the car."

Tracy unlatched the door and entered the cage. Holly saw the dog try to push his body deeper into the corner as

Tracy approached. She stooped down to pick him up and put him in the carrier.

When they reached the car, Holly opened the back door, and Tracy placed the carrier on the back seat. Matt slid in next to it.

Tracy turned to Holly. "Call me tomorrow to let me know how he's doing, okay?"

"I will," Holly said, and gave Tracy a hug.

The sun was down, and at six o'clock, it was as dark as it would get that night. Holly started the engine and opened the car window to say good-bye to Tracy. "Thanks again for all your help."

Tracy bent down and looked in at Toby's new family. "You're welcome, and don't forget, call me tomorrow."

"I will," Holly promised, and backed the car out of the parking space.

Matt waved through the rear window as the car pulled away. Tracy waved back and watched until the bright red taillights vanished around the bend in the road.

Holly turned toward the empty passenger seat next to her. "How's he doing back there?" she asked Matt.

"I don't know. I can't see him. I think he's okay."

"He'll feel better when we get him settled in at home," said Holly. At least, I hope he will, she thought to herself. Inwardly, she wasn't so sure.

Matt sat back in his seat with his arm protectively on top of the carrier. He couldn't wait for his friends to see his new dog. They were going to be so jealous!

As Holly drove, doubts and misgivings whirled through

her mind. Where would the dog sleep? Would he like the food they had bought for him? Was he housebroken? How could she have forgotten to ask Tracy all of these questions? She took a deep breath and slowly exhaled. Everything would work out. It had to.

CHAPTER 31

HOLLY PULLED THE car into the driveway. Matt unhooked his seatbelt just as his mother turned off the engine. She held out the house keys to him.

"Go in and shut the bedroom doors. I have a feeling that when we bring Marshmallow in the house he's going to try to find a corner to hide in. We don't want him to end up underneath one of the beds."

Matt took the keys from his mother and ran up the stone path to the front door. He quickly opened it and turned on the porch light. Sandy, their orange tabby cat, sprang out the door and ran into the darkness of the backyard. Matt knew they wouldn't see him again until the next morning. Sandy liked to prowl the neighborhood at night. Occasionally he would bring back a souvenir of his adventures. The last time he had brought back a dead mole.

Holly got out of the car and opened the back door. She peered into the slats of the carrier. Through the dim light of the car's overhead bulb she saw the sad brown eyes that had haunted her the past two weeks looking up at her.

She picked up the carrier and carefully made her way up the stone path to the back of the building where the only entrance to their little house faced the large field behind the property. Moonlight cast an unearthly glow on the expanse of land that stretched out from the edge of the back yard to where it met the woods in the distance.

Holly turned the corner of the building and carefully climbed up the stairs guided by the illumination of the porch light. Matt opened the door when she reached the top step.

"Did you close the bedroom doors?" Holly asked, as she entered the house.

"Yup, and I closed the bathroom door."

"Good."

Holly placed the carrier on the living room rug and unlatched the small plastic door. She peered in at Toby. He seemed smaller and more vulnerable than he had at the kennel. She slowly slid her hands under each side of his body, feeling the soft, downy fur for the first time. She pulled him forward and lifted him out of the carrier. He wasn't as heavy as she thought he would be. She could hear his fast, shallow breathing and feel the quick rise and fall of his chest against her own.

Holly gingerly placed Toby on the carpet and sat down on the floor beside him. He remained still, watching her every move. With long, slow caresses, she stroked the fur down his back to comfort him, but each time she placed her hand upon the soft whiteness, he flinched. Matt knelt down on the other side of him and tentatively patted the top of his head. Toby's eyes nervously moved back and forth between them like a nervous tick over which he had no control.

"He still looks scared, Ma."

"I know. He's going to need time. Even a dog that hasn't been abused needs time to adjust. Why don't we leave him alone for a little while. I'll start supper while you go get the things out of the trunk."

✧ ✧ ✧

TOBY LAY STILL on the soft carpet. Where was he now? Who were these people? He felt vulnerable lying out in the open floor, so as soon as the woman and the boy left the room, he scurried under a small table in the corner.

✧ ✧ ✧

"MA!" MATT CRIED out in excitement when he came back into the house carrying the bags from the pet store. Holly quickly turned from the sink where she was washing lettuce. Matt pointed with his free hand into the living room. The dog was gone!

"Where did he go?" she asked in alarm.

"He's under the end table in the corner!"

Holly moved back from the sink and peered around the corner of the living room. There he was, scrunched beneath the small table. She brought one of her wet hands up to her chest and sighed.

Matt set the bags down on the floor and went over to Toby. "I guess you were right, Ma. First thing he wanted to do was find a corner to lie in. Maybe we should put his bed under there for him," he suggested.

"That's a good idea," said Holly, who had moved back to the sink to continue shaking the water out of the lettuce. A knock on the door startled her. She turned to see her landlord, Mrs. Sullivan, standing under the glow of the porch light.

"Come on in, Mrs. Sullivan," Holly called out.

Mrs. Sullivan, a statuesque woman in her early fifties, had been an only child and was the sole heir of her parent's considerable estate. She hadn't worked in years and was almost always home when the bus dropped Matt off after school. Holly thought of her more as a friend than as a landlord.

"Did you pick up the dog yet?" Mrs. Sullivan asked.

"He's over in the corner next to Matt."

Mrs. Sullivan went over to where Matt sat on the floor in front of the end table.

"Hi, Matt, who have you got there?" She peered around Matt's body to get a view of the dog.

"Hi, Mrs. Sullivan," Matt said, and shifted over so she could see the dog better. "This is Marshmallow!"

She knelt on the floor and looked under the table.

"Oh!" she exclaimed. "He's absolutely beautiful!" She turned and looked up at Holly standing behind her. "What kind of dog is he?"

"He's a German Shepherd mix."

Mrs. Sullivan looked back down at Toby. "I've never seen a dog so white before. His fur almost glows! And his eyes, they look so sad, poor thing. Do you think it would help if I brought Bailey over?" Bailey was a 95-pound yellow Labrador Retriever, who had a heart of gold but didn't realize how big and strong he was. Every time he saw Holly, he jumped up and tried to lick her face. Holly knew he was only trying to be friendly, but she was afraid he was going to knock her down one day.

"Maybe we should wait a little while before we introduce the puppy to Bailey," Holly suggested. "He seems pretty scared right now." Holly hoped Mrs. Sullivan wouldn't push the issue. At times she could be very persistent.

"I suppose you're right," said Mrs. Sullivan. "But Bailey's going to be tickled pink when he finally meets Marshmallow."

"Ma and I decided we're going to give him a new name," Matt said. "We're just waiting to get to know him better before we pick one."

Mrs. Sullivan studied Toby for a moment. "I can see why you'd want to change that name. Marshmallow doesn't fit him at all. Not at all," she pronounced, and pushed herself up off the floor. "Well, I can see you're making dinner, so I'll let you get on with it." Before she reached the door, she turned back to Holly. "You've never had a dog before, have you?"

Holly shook her head. "No, and I never thought I would. This is all new to me."

"Well, feel free to call me if you have any questions or need any help, okay?"

"I do have one question," Holly said just before Mrs. Sullivan reached the door. "How often should we take him out to go to the bathroom?"

Mrs. Sullivan turned back to Holly.

"Is he housebroken?"

"It didn't occur to me to ask. I just assumed he was."

"He looks old enough to be housebroken. How old is he?"

"The woman at the humane society thought he was about seven months old."

"Then he's probably already trained. If he is, your life will be a lot easier; if he isn't, you'll have to train him." Mrs. Sullivan saw a look of dismay drape Holly's face and quickly said, "Let's assume he is. You'll know soon enough. He should be taken out first thing in the morning, then once in the afternoon, and then again after supper and before bedtime."

"That doesn't sound so bad," Holly said with a sigh of relief. "I was wondering what I was going to do if he had to be taken out when no one was here, but it sounds like he should be okay until Matt gets home from school."

"He should be. But if you ever need me to help you out, let me know. I'd be glad to."

"You're an angel, Mrs. Sullivan."

"Oh, it's nothing. I'm right next door." Her landlord opened the door to leave. "I'll stop by tomorrow to see how he's doing."

"Okay. Thanks for coming over."

Holly watched her go down the steps and across the yard before turning off the porch light and closing the door against the cold night air.

Later that evening Matt lay sprawled in his pajamas on the floor in front of Toby. Holly had placed his dog bed under the table after taking him out of the corner for a moment.

"He still looks scared," Matt said to his mother, who sat on the couch reading. She looked up from the newspaper.

"Do you think he'll get up and eat soon?" Matt asked.

"He'll probably wait until we go to bed to eat. And speaking of bed, it's about that time."

Matt scrunched up his face. "Can't I stay up a little longer?"

Holly looked over at the wall clock.

"It's almost ten o'clock. You've already been up close to an hour past your bedtime. You'll have plenty of time to spend with him tomorrow after school," Holly said with finality, cutting off Matt's unspoken protest.

After Holly settled Matt in bed, she went back into the living room. She looked over at the kitchen. Dirty supper dishes still sat on the table waiting to be washed. They could wait, she thought, and she sat on the floor opposite Toby, who watched her every move from under the table. She looked into his eyes. Trepidation suddenly filled her. All of the misgivings she had so successfully suppressed rose to the surface again. The realization hit her that the animal sitting in the corner of her living room was completely dependent on her. His life was in her hands. I must have been crazy to take him, she thought. I don't know a thing about dogs. What was I thinking?

The minutes ticked away. Their eyes remained locked. Then slowly, amidst the uncertainty of her fears, the strength of her resolve reemerged. Somehow she would break through the walls the dog had erected around himself. Somehow the strength of her love for him would defeat the fear that held him in its grip.

Through the haze of sleep, Holly felt someone shaking her arm. Groaning, she rolled away from the annoyance and pulled the comforter over her head.

"Ma, wake up!" Matt shook her arm again. "Marshmallow ate all his food!"

Holly sat up in bed and tried to focus on her son through the dim morning light of the bedroom. "What?"

"The dog food bowl is empty. Marshmallow ate his food! Come see!"

Holly climbed out of bed, grabbed her bathrobe, and followed Matt down the hall to the kitchen.

"He must have gotten up while we were sleeping," Holly said. "I'd better take him outside to go to the bathroom."

"Can I come?" Matt asked.

"Sure, but put on your coat and sneakers. It's chilly out." Matt ran into his room and came back out to find his mother hooking the new red leash onto Toby's collar. She gently urged him out from under the table and led him to the front door, which she opened with her free hand to the wintry morning air. Sandy, who had been waiting on the porch to come in, ran past them into the house and disappeared down the hall.

"I wonder what Sandy will think of the dog." Holly mused. "I hope they get along okay."

"They will. They'll become good friends," Matt said with certainty.

Holly smiled and stepped out onto the porch.

✧   ✧   ✧

TOBY HAD BEEN startled by the orange tabby cat who had dashed past him into the house earlier that morning, though he had immediately detected the cat's scent the night before. Now the cat was nowhere to be seen. The boy and the woman had left the house earlier, and all was quiet and still. He laid his head back down between his paws and contemplated his situation, but the events of the past two days had emotionally and physically drained him, and he soon fell asleep.

The sound was barely audible at first; just a faint murmur. Then it was gone. Toby turned in his sleep.

"I don't think he heard you," a voice said.

"Toby, can you hear me?" said another.

Toby shifted again.

"I think he's coming around."

"Toby?"

The familiar voices drifted into Toby's slumbering mind. A warmth from the happy memories they elicited filled his being. Recognition brought him awake. He opened his eyes and beheld his sister and best friend standing before him. Joy sprang from his heart.

"Tara! Drake! Are you really here? I've missed you both so much!"

"We've missed you too, Toby."

"How do you know each other?" Toby asked with bewildered excitement.

"In this world, everyone knows each other, my good friend," Drake replied. "Don't ask me how, for I would not be able to explain it to you in terms you would understand. Your sister and I met almost immediately after . . . well, let's not talk about that."

"I'm just so happy to see you both!"

"Are you happy otherwise, Toby?" Tara gently asked.

Toby looked down. His joy had been pierced by one

simple question. He looked up again. *"How can I ever be truly happy again when I've lost you both?"*

"You haven't lost us, Toby," Tara assured him. *"We are with you now and always will be, both in memory and in spirit. No one can take us from you. As you will always love us, we will always love you. But we want you to open up your heart to your new family as they have opened up theirs to you. Promise us you will try to do that, will you, Toby?"*

Toby slowly nodded his head and closed his eyes, which had begun to well with tears. The part of him that fought the idea of giving himself over to love again had begun to crumble even before their spectral visit. Now his self-constructed wall of emotional isolation crumbled further under the weight of their concern. He would open himself up to love again, he decided, even as his dream began to fade, along with the vision of Tara and Drake.

Toby woke up with a renewed spirit; the images of Tara and Drake still freshly with him, as well as the promise he had made.

He stood up and stretched. The house was quiet and still. He headed to the kitchen for a drink of water.

"Who are you?" a voice asked from behind him.

Startled, Toby turned and found himself face to face with the orange tabby.

"Do you go around scaring everyone like that?" Toby asked, trying to subdue the trembling caused by the sudden fright.

"Sorry," said the cat, considering Toby through the

narrow black slits of his deep golden eyes. *"I didn't mean to scare you."*

The cat reminded Toby of Cookie, Shelby's mom. Remembering what Meesha and Pinka had done for him, he pushed aside his initial instinct to dislike the cat.

"My name's Sandy," the cat continued. *"What's yours?"*

"Toby."

"Are you a friend of Bailey's?"

"Who's Bailey?"

"The dog next door," said Sandy. *"Haven't you met him yet?"*

"No. I didn't know a dog lived next door. Is he friendly?" Toby asked.

"Yeah, he's pretty harmless, though every once in a while he gets loose and chases me into the woods. I always manage to lose him, though. I'm sure the two of you will get along just fine."

"How long have you lived here?" Toby asked.

"A couple of years. I lived with the woman and the boy a couple of other places before we moved here. I like this place the best. There are more things to explore and fewer people around."

"Do you like living with the woman and the boy?"

"Sure. They're my family. They treat me well and take good care of me. What about you? Where did you live before?"

Toby hesitated before answering. *"I lived in a couple of different places, too."*

Just then they heard footsteps on the porch, and the storm door opened.

"The boy's home," Sandy announced. "We'll talk again later." He ran over to the door, which opened with a flourish, barely missing the cat as he bolted outside.

Toby did not wait to see who came through the door. He sprinted to his corner and into his bed just as the boy entered the house.

✧ ✧ ✧

"SO MATT," HOLLY said, interrupting her son's thoughts later that night as they finished eating dinner. "Do you want to pick a name for the dog after we clean up the supper dishes?"

"Sure!" Matt shoved the last bite of his spaghetti into his mouth. He jumped up and helped his mother clear off the table and clean up the kitchen with more enthusiasm than usual. A few minutes later, they sat on the living room floor next to Toby.

"What's your first choice?" Holly asked, fully expecting to hear the name Rocket shoot out of her son's mouth.

"Duke," Matt said, without hesitation.

"Duke," Holly repeated the name. "That's a nice solid name. I like it."

"What's your first pick?" Matt asked his mother.

"I have two. One is Ripley, which I thought of because when I was about your age, a friend of mine had a dog named Ripley."

"Ripley's cool. What's the other one?"

"Well, other than Ripley, I couldn't think of any other name that felt right for him until I was driving home from work and a name came to me from out of the blue."

"What name?" Matt asked impatiently.

"Toby."

"Toby." Matt slowly repeated the name.

"What do you think?" his mother asked.

Matt looked over at the white dog curled underneath the end table, then said, "He kind of looks like a Toby, huh?"

Holly leaned over and looked past Matt at the dog.

Holly sat back up. "The name does fit him," she said.

Matt looked up at his mother then back at the dog and said, "Welcome to your new home, Toby."

Holly smiled.

CHAPTER 32

TOBY CAME OUT from under his table the next morning after the woman and boy had left the house.

"Good morning, Toby," said Sandy, who stood in the kitchen at the water bowl.

"Good morning," Toby replied.

"Did you have a good sleep?" the cat asked.

"Yes, thank you. Where do you sleep?" he asked the cat.

"I sleep in the boy's room on his bed. You haven't been in there yet, have you?"

"No."

"Come on. I'll take you on a tour."

Toby thought twice and then followed the cat down the short hallway into the boy's room at the front of the house. Sandy deftly jumped up onto the bed that was pushed up against a wall that had two windows in it side by side.

"Come on up," he urged Toby.

"Are you sure it's okay?"

"Sure. Jump up, and we can each have a window to look out of."

Toby hesitated and then leapt up onto the soft, cushiony bed. The cat lay down at the window at the far end of the bed and Toby tentatively lay down next to the other window. From their vantage point they could see part of the road in front of the house and the woods beyond. Toby began to relax as the two passed the day talking and sleeping and looking out the window. Every now and then a car would drive by and they would stop their conversation to watch it pass. Toward mid-afternoon Sandy rose and stretched out her legs. A moment later a large vehicle pulled up in front of the house.

"The boy's home," Sandy said, and without preamble, jumped off the bed and sprinted down the hall. Toby followed.

Just as he settled into his corner, Toby heard the sounds of the boy running up the porch steps, followed by the key unlocking the door. Sandy darted through the door as soon as it opened. The boy entered and swung the large bag slung over his shoulder onto the kitchen table; it landed with a thud. Grabbing the leash off the hook next to the door, he approached Toby.

It was time to go out again. Toby looked forward to going out with the boy, who usually walked him around the back yard so he could smell all the wonderful and unusual scents. The scent of another dog, assuredly Bailey's, pervaded the area. He wondered when he would meet Bailey. It would be nice to make a new friend.

Toby followed the boy down the porch stairs and into the yard.

Just then, a door slammed and a huge dog, the color of Sandy, but lighter, bounded across the yard toward Toby and the boy; a long blue leash trailing behind him. A woman appeared from around the corner of the house frantically trying to catch up with the dog. That must be Bailey, Toby thought. He's huge!

Bailey rushed upon Toby, who turned to make a dash back to the porch.

"Hey! Don't run away!" Bailey implored, just as he reached Toby and came to a sudden stop. "I'm not going to hurt you. I just want to say hello and introduce myself."

Toby stopped and warily turned toward the larger dog. He gave Bailey a dubious look.

"My name's Bailey. What's yours?"

"Toby."

"Hi, Toby! I was hoping we'd meet soon. I've smelled your scent for the past few days and saw you out the window yesterday. I haven't had a friend to play with since the last people who lived in your house moved."

Toby immediately liked this gregarious dog.

"I've smelled your scent too," said Toby. "Sandy told me a little bit about you."

"He probably told you I chase him every now and then, but it's all in good fun. I'd never hurt him. Besides, he always gets away by running into the bushes."

Toby smiled inside as the older dog continued.

"I hope we have a lot of chances to play and explore together."

"Where do you go exploring?" Toby asked.

"Oh, there are plenty of places to investigate around here. Of course," Bailey dropped his voice and continued

more quietly, *"We have to be able to get away from the yard to do any really good exploring."*

"How do you get away from the yard?" Toby asked.

"If you run fast enough and catch whoever is holding the leash off guard, they usually can't hold on, and off you go!" said Bailey with unbridled enthusiasm, just as the woman picked up the end of Bailey's leash.

"Aren't you ever afraid you're going to get lost?"

"Nah, I know my way around here. There are lots of trails in the woods to explore, and sometimes, if I'm lucky, the deer are passing through the field and I get to chase them!"

"What do you do when you catch them?

"I haven't had to decide yet since I've never caught one. They run pretty fast. But it's fun trying!"

Toby wasn't sure about the deer chasing part, but running free in the woods sounded like fun.

The woman, who'd been talking with the boy, tugged on Bailey's leash and tried to pull him away from Toby.

"It's suppertime for me!" Bailey said. "I hope we get to see each other again soon so we can play or explore together or maybe even chase some deer! See you later!"

"Bye," Toby said, as he watched his new friend disappear with the woman around the corner of the house next door. The warmth of a new friendship filled him.

✧ ✧ ✧

THE SKY HUNG HEAVY with leaden clouds as Holly drove home, giving the appearance that it was later in the day than it was. The first storm of the season was predicted to begin early that evening and continue into the next day.

When Holly entered the house, Matt came running out from his bedroom.

"Hi, Ma!"

"Hi, Matt. How was school today?"

"Good. Guess what?"

"What?"

"When I took Toby out to go to the bathroom after school, Mrs. Sullivan came outside with Bailey and Toby and Bailey got to meet each other!"

"That's great! How did they get along? Was Toby afraid of Bailey?"

"At first he seemed to be, but after they sniffed each other for a few minutes, Toby didn't seem afraid anymore."

"I hope you had Toby on the leash."

"I did. He tried to pull away when Bailey came running over, but I held on tight."

"We need to be careful. You know how Bailey likes to take off sometimes. I don't know if Toby would follow him, but we don't want to take any chances."

"Don't worry, Ma. I'll hold on to the leash really tight when I take him out," assured Matt.

"Good," Holly said, as she took off her coat and threw it on the couch. She squatted down next to the end table. "Hi, Toby. You had an exciting day today, didn't you?" She stroked the top of his head. "I'm glad you made a doggie friend." She continued to pet Toby, as she said to Matt, "Did you know we're supposed to get a big snow storm tonight?"

"We are?" Matt asked excitedly. "Maybe there won't be any school tomorrow!"

"Probably not, the way the weatherman was talking. He said we could get up to a foot of snow."

"Yippee!" Matt cried out.

"I wouldn't celebrate yet. They seem to be wrong at least half the time."

The next morning Matt jumped out of bed and ran to the window. He grabbed the bottom of the shade and yanked it up. The world before him was blanketed in white. It was hard to determine how deep the snow was, but it sure looked deep enough to keep him out of school for the day!

Matt heard the sound of the shower running in the bathroom. He glanced up at the clock next to his bed. The time was past when his mother usually woke him. He ran to the partially opened bathroom door and yelled in, "Hey, Ma, did school get canceled?'

"Yes it did!" she yelled back from behind the shower curtain. "There's already four inches of snow, and they're expecting up to six more by the end of the day."

"Yahoo!" Matt cried out, and then asked, "Did your work get canceled?"

He heard his mother laugh. "No. We'd have to get twelve feet before they'd cancel work."

Matt was elated. Freshly fallen snow with more to come, no school, and the house to himself all day! He couldn't wait to call his friend Jimmy. Jimmy lived on the road on the other side of the woods behind the field. The previous summer they had found a small path that they used as a shortcut to each other's houses. Jimmy hadn't seen his new dog yet. He turned on the television and sat down on the floor next to Toby.

"Make sure you eat a good breakfast before you go outside and dress warm. It's only twenty-five degrees out," Holly told Matt, as she put on her coat to leave for work. "And don't forget to take Toby out at lunchtime, and shovel the porch and the sidewalk. You might have to shovel more than once."

"I will, Ma. Don't worry. I know what to do."

Holly went over to Toby and bent down. "You have a good day, too, Toby," she said, as she stroked the top of his head.

"Okay. I'm leaving now. Call me if you need me." Holly bent down and gave Matt a kiss goodbye. "Have fun today, and if you go over to anyone's house, let me know, okay?"

"I will, Ma," Matt promised, and followed his mother to lock the door behind her as she headed out into the storm.

Matt turned the deadbolt and ran into his bedroom. He watched his mother brush the snow off the car and waved as she pulled out of the driveway. Once her car was out of sight, he ran into the kitchen to call Jimmy.

The snow was wet and heavy, perfect for making snowballs. Jimmy's younger brother Curtis and his friend Troy were coming over for a snowball fight after lunch. Matt couldn't wait.

He had almost finished shoveling the back walk—though new snow had already accumulated enough to obscure his efforts—when he heard Jimmy yelling behind him. He turned to see his friend trudging through the snow-covered field towing a bright orange sled behind him.

"Hey, Matt!"

"Hey, Jimmy!" Matt yelled. "I'll be right there!" He tossed the last load of heavy snow onto the large mound he had created, pushed the shovel head deep into the pile, and ran through the snow to meet Jimmy.

"Isn't this great!" Matt let out a loud whoop and dropped to the ground, rolling in the snow and tossing handfuls of the white stuff up into the air. Jimmy let go of the rope attached to his sled and joined Matt. The two boys laughed as they threw snow at each other.

"Do you want to see Toby?"

"Yeah!" Jimmy said. They jumped up and ran to the house as fast as the deepening snow allowed.

When the two boys reached the porch, they took off their boots and brushed the snow off their jackets and pants. Once inside, Matt pointed to the corner of the living room. "There he is," he said with a note of pride in his voice.

"Wow! He's all white!"

"Isn't he cool looking?"

"Yeah! Can I pet him?"

"Sure. But walk over to him slowly. He gets scared easily."

"What's he afraid of?"

"The woman at the Humane Society said he was abused by the man who had him before us."

"You mean the man hurt him?"

"Yeah," Matt said solemnly, as he sat down in front of the end table.

"That's sad," said Jimmy, as he knelt down beside his friend and cautiously placed his hand on Toby's soft fur. He felt a shudder travel down the dog's back.

"He's so soft and white," Jimmy exclaimed. "He's as white as the snow! I bet you wouldn't be able to see him if he were outside!"

Jimmy continued to stroke Toby's fur. After a few moments, Matt stood up. "Let's go back out and make some ammunition before lunch. I can't wait for Curtis and Troy to get here. We're gonna wallop them in the snowball fight!"

Just as Matt and Jimmy finished their sandwiches, the doorbell rang. Matt pulled the curtain back and saw Curtis peering through the window at him.

"We'll be out in a minute!" Matt yelled through the glass. Curtis nodded and trudged back down the porch steps.

Matt quickly picked up the luncheon remains from the kitchen table and placed the dishes in the sink. His mother wouldn't be happy if she came home to dirty dishes, but he was anxious to start the snowball fight.

"Can Toby come out, too?" Jimmy asked.

"I almost forgot. I have to take him out to go to the bathroom," Matt said, as he finished putting his snow gear back on. He grabbed the leash from the hook and went over to Toby's corner. Once he had the leash hooked onto the collar, he gently tugged at it several times. Toby reluctantly crawled out from under the table and stood on the rug. Matt pulled him toward the door.

"I think he's afraid of you," Matt commented. "He usually likes to go out."

"I'm a little afraid of him, too," Jimmy admitted. "He's a lot bigger than he seemed when he was under the table."

Curtis and Troy stopped playing when they saw Matt come out of the house with the dog.

"Whose dog is that?" Curtis asked.

"Mine," Matt replied proudly. "His name's Toby."

"Where'd you get him?"

"At the Humane Society."

"Is he friendly?"

"He's a little scared because he was abused."

"Can I pet him?" Curtis asked.

"Sure."

Curtis walked up to Toby and put his hand out. Toby backed away.

"He's afraid of me," Curtis said.

"I'm sure he'll let you pet him once he gets to know you better," Matt said, and tugged at the leash. "Come on, Toby. Time to go to the bathroom."

Curtis watched the dog follow behind Matt as he led him to the side of the house.

✧ ✧ ✧

TOBY FOLLOWED *the boy outside. For a moment, he experienced a feeling of déjà vu. Snow was falling, covering the entire landscape within his view. The air, cold and crisp as it entered his lungs, exited in a cloud of steam that slowly floated among the gently swirling flakes. His dream of running through the snow-covered tundra with his grandfather and the pack came back to him with such vivid clarity that he fully expected to see them dashing through the field behind the house.*

As the boy led him down the porch stairs, Toby's paws left deep, dimpled impressions in the soft snow. Large, wet flakes alighted on his nose and accumulated on his fur. The world was a white wonderland. His dream, a reality before him.

CHAPTER 33

BAILEY STOOD AT the back door and barked. Mrs. Sullivan reluctantly rose from the kitchen table and set the newspaper down next to her half-eaten sandwich.

"You want to go out *again*, Bailey? You were just out an hour ago."

Bailey barked once more, his tail wagging enthusiastically.

"Okay. Okay. I'll let you out."

She noticed Matt's friends playing in the snow as she passed the window in the family room.

"I see. You want to go out and play with the boys, don't you?" On occasion, she would let Bailey outside to play with Matt and his friends in the back yard. They threw his ball to him, or sticks, or anything else Bailey was willing to fetch.

"You can go out for a few minutes, but no running away this time!" she admonished, as she opened the back door.

As soon as Bailey heard the latch click, he pushed against the storm door and bolted outside.

Matt held onto Toby's leash as he watched Curtis and Troy make snowballs for their arsenal. They'd better work fast, he thought. He eyed the large pile of snow balls Jimmy and he had made before lunch. He wished Toby could stay out and play with them. Maybe next winter.

Matt heard the muted sound of Bailey barking from inside Mrs. Sullivan's house. Toby barked back. It was the first time he had heard Toby bark!

"Good boy, Toby! That's your new friend Bailey."

Toby barked again.

This time Bailey's responding bark was much louder and clearer. A moment later, Matt saw why, as Bailey bounded around the corner of the house.

"HI, TOBY!" Bailey cried out, stopping just short of plowing into his new friend.

"Hi, Bailey!" Toby responded, quickly overcoming his startle at the older dog's sudden appearance.

"Don't you just love the snow?" Bailey asked, and stuck his nose several inches into a deep drift the wind had sculpted against the house.

"This is the first time I've seen snow," Toby said. "I had a dream about it, though."

"Dreaming about it can't be as good as the real thing,"

Bailey claimed. "This would be a great day to go exploring. What do you say?"

"I don't know. . ." Toby paused, then asked, "Are you sure it's safe?"

"What could happen?"

"What if we get lost?"

"We won't. I know my way around. I've been up and down every trail in the area. Besides, we won't be going near any streets or houses. Come, on. It'll be fun!"

The same exhilarated feeling that Toby had experienced in his dream filled him again. To experience that same joy for real! That sense of total freedom. The feel of the wind and snow rushing past as he effortlessly flew across the landscape like a bird unfettered by the earth's gravity.

"But how can I get away from the boy? He's holding the end of the leash."

"It's easy," Bailey said. "You just need to pull the leash out of his grasp. I do it all the time. When he starts back up the porch stairs, we'll make a hard dash toward the field. He'll have to let go. And then you'll be free!"

Toby wasn't confident the scheme would work. He wasn't sure he wanted it to work. What if the boy got mad at him? What if they did get lost in the snow enshrouded woods? But what if the plan did work? Toby's misgivings succumbed to his desire to run free.

✧ ✧ ✧

MATT GRIPPED the end of Toby's leash as tight as his bulky mittens would allow and waited while the two dogs sniffed each other. Toby was happy to see Bailey. His tail wagged as the two interacted, but the snowball fight awaited, and after a few minutes, Matt gently tugged at Toby's leash to lead him back to the house.

As he started up the porch steps, thoughts of the upcoming snow ball fight filled him with excitement.

✧ ✧ ✧

JUST AS BAILEY was about to yell for Toby to run, the boy slipped on the top step of the porch and landed on the snow covered deck.

Toby looked up and saw the end of the leash lying on the snow next to the boy.

"Run, Toby!" Bailey shouted, and took off in the direction of the woods.

Toby looked over at his friend and then back at the boy who was now reaching out to pick up the leash.

Toby ran.

He was free.

Just as Toby reached Bailey at the edge of the field, he heard the boy yell his name. He turned. The boy was frantically running toward them. Toby paused.

"Come on, Toby!" Bailey yelled. "Let's go!"

Toby turned back toward Bailey and once more to the boy. He took off.

The wind whistled in his ears. The snow pelted his face. Any physical and emotional restraint he had felt previously was gone. The gray and white blur of the surroundings flew past him. The elation he had felt in his dream filled his body and soul. Bailey led them to the far end of the field where the woods began, and without slowing down, turned right into the dense trees. Toby followed and found himself on a wide path. He caught up to Bailey, and the two wayfarers continued on side-by-side.

Toby didn't know how long they ran before his lungs began to burn. He slowed his pace just as Bailey suddenly veered left into a thicket of trees. As Toby approached the point where his friend had vanished, he noticed a narrow path just wide enough for one. He followed Bailey deeper into the woods. Parts of the narrow trail were obstructed by tree trunks and branches and twigs that had fallen prey to old age or to the weather. In some places, they were forced to gingerly find their way over or around the larger obstacles they encountered.

"Can we stop for a minute, Bailey?" Toby's voice broke the silence.

"Sure," Bailey replied. "I'm getting kind of tired myself. And I'm thirsty. There's a small stream a little farther up we might be able to get a drink from if it isn't frozen over."

At the mention of the stream, Toby's mouth suddenly felt dry.

"How far is it?" Toby asked.

"It's only a couple of minutes from here. If we go directly through the woods, it'll be faster. Follow me." Bailey stepped off the path and into the snow covered undergrowth that blanketed the forest floor. Toby followed.

✧　✧　✧

THE LEASH slipped from Matt's grasp as he put his hands out to break his fall. He landed with a soft thud on the snow-covered wooden planks of the porch deck.

Momentarily stunned, he didn't notice the end of Toby's leash lying next to him in the snow until it was too late. He watched helplessly as it leapt beyond his reach and swiftly trailed away behind Toby, like a red snake gliding over the fresh impressions left by the two dogs in the snow.

"Toby! Come back!" Matt yelled, as he ran down the stairs and in the direction the two dogs had taken flight. Their images, blurred by the thickening snow that blew into his eyes, vanished into the storm.

Jimmy, now only steps behind him, yelled to Matt, "I'll help you find him. I told Curtis and Troy to stay behind in case the dogs come back while we're looking for them."

Running as fast as the deepening snow would allow, the two boys followed the dogs' trail.

CHAPTER 34

BAILEY CAREFULLY picked his way through the leafless branches and boughs of the dense undergrowth.

Toby followed.

"We're almost there," Bailey shouted back to Toby. "I can hear the water."

Toby jumped over a dead tree that interrupted Bailey's trail in the snow.

Suddenly, he was jerked to a stop.

He turned his head and saw that the loop at the end of the leash had caught around a large branch of the fallen tree. He pulled to no avail. The branch held the leash firmly in its grip just as the panic rising in Toby held him. He peered through the falling snow. Bailey was nowhere in sight.

"Bailey!" Toby yelled in the direction of the stream. "I'm stuck!"

Bailey had just reached the edge of the water when he heard his friend call out.

"I'm coming, Toby!" he yelled back.

MATT AND JIMMY followed the dogs' tracks, which were now no more than dents in the smooth blanket of snow. Sweat began to accumulate on Matt's skin. A quarter of a mile or so down the trail, the tracks turned into the woods down one of the many narrow footpaths that sinuously wove their way through the dense trees.

✧   ✧   ✧

BAILEY REACHED TOBY and immediately saw the problem. His friend's leash was caught on the branch of a dead tree.

Toby was firmly trapped in place.

"What are we going to do, Bailey?" asked Toby. "The more I try to free myself, the more stuck I get."

"Don't worry," Bailey assured the younger dog. He could see they would need one of the humans to help unravel the leash from its stranglehold. "I'll go back and get help."

"Don't leave me, Bailey," Toby implored.

"Don't be scared. And don't try to move again. I'll be right back."

Toby watched Bailey make his way back through the underbrush. His body began to tremble.

"I'm never going to run away again," Toby promised himself and the silent trees standing guard around him. "I just want to go home."

Bailey broke through the woods onto the foot path and ran back to the carriage road. Through the wind in his ears, he thought her heard someone yell Toby's name.

"Toby! Where are you?"

He heard it more clearly this time. It was the boy.

Bailey began to bark.

✧　✧　✧

MATT SUDDENLY stopped.

"Did you hear that?" he yelled to Jimmy.

Jimmy stopped a few yards ahead and pulled the knit cap off his head.

The barking sounded again.

"It's Bailey!" Matt cried. "It's coming from the direction of the stream. Come on!"

The boys ran through the thickening snowfall. Just as they reached a curve in the trail, Bailey came bounding around the bend almost running them down. He stopped and quickly turned back in the direction he had just come, barking at Matt and Jimmy to follow.

Mrs. Sullivan opened the back door to check on Bailey and saw two of Matt's friends standing at the edge of the field facing the woods.

"Bailey!" she called out into the cold. Snow flew past her into the house.

The two boys turned.

"Bailey and Toby ran away," one of the boys yelled at her. "Matt and Jimmy are looking for them."

Oh no, not again, Mrs. Sullivan thought to herself. And Toby. Toby doesn't know his way around. She ran to the coat closet in the front entrance hall to get her parka and snow boots.

CHAPTER 35

TOBY HEARD BAILEY'S bark in the distance. His body trembled from the cold wetness that had soaked through his fur and settled on his skin. He wasn't sure if it was fear or cold or both that caused his uncontrollable shuddering.

Bailey barked again. Closer this time.

He was coming back!

Had the boy followed him? Was he with Bailey?

A few moments later Bailey was by his side.

"Bailey, thank goodness! Did you find the boy? Is he coming to help?"

"The boy and his friend are right behind me," Bailey said with labored breaths. "They'll be here any minute."

Relief surged through Toby, but the shivering that firmly gripped him continued, even after he saw the boy emerge through the snow.

✧   ✧   ✧

BAILEY BOLTED ahead of the two boys and faded into the thickening snowfall.

"Bailey!" Matt called out. "Wait up!" But the dog had vanished, and now all they could do was follow his trail.

After a few minutes, the trail stopped and turned off the path into the woods.

They heard Bailey bark.

The two boys ran toward the sound while pushing aside small saplings and tangled twigs and boughs of the thick underbrush.

Bailey barked again. They were close.

The images of the two dogs materialized through the snow.

Matt ran toward them. As he got closer, he could see Toby's entangled red leash. When he reached Toby, he dropped to his knees and wrapped his arms around him. Tears welled in his eyes. Toby licked his face. The tears fell.

"Toby, don't ever run away again! You scared me to death!" Matt held the trembling wet body against him. Toby didn't resist.

EPILOGUE

HOLLY SMILED AS she watched Ripley patiently wait for the squirrel that had just run up the tree trunk to come back down. Little did he know the squirrel had probably already left the yard jumping from branch to branch, from tree to tree. She leaned over the sink and could just see Toby lying on the deck. The ten years since they adopted Toby had passed quickly. They now lived in their own home not far from the little apartment over Mrs. Sullivan's garage. Matt attended college at the local university and was studying Sports Management. He would be graduating the following spring. Holly wasn't exactly sure what kind of job he might be able to get once he graduated, but that didn't matter. He was following his bliss and from there he would find his way.

They had adopted Ripley several years earlier; a purebred white German Shepherd they had rescued after he had been found wandering homeless by a woman at their veterinarian's office. Holly didn't necessarily believe in fate—one had to take responsibility for directing one's life—but when she had seen Ripley that day, she knew there was also a greater force at work.

✧ ✧ ✧

TOBY LAY ON the warm wooden planks of the deck and watched as Ripley chased a squirrel up one of the old oak trees in the back yard. The younger dog jumped up and placed his front paws on the wide trunk, then barked several times to let the squirrel know who was boss. Toby smiled inside.

The sun felt good. Arthritis had begun to gradually set into his joints over the past year, especially in the leg the man had injured; but the pain was bearable, and he could still get around. He couldn't keep up with Ripley anymore, but then, he never really could.

Toby knew the time was drawing near when he would have to leave this life, but he was not afraid. His loved ones who had already made the journey would be waiting for him; his mother and Drake and Tara. And he would leave this world with no regrets, taking with him the memories of years filled with love and happiness.

As he lay there, he reflected back on the dream that had changed his life. The dream in which Drake and Tara had made him promise that he would open his heart to love again; to give his new family a chance. He had kept that promise and had found love again. He had found a place he felt safe and secure. A place where he was happy and content. A place to call home . . .

CPSIA information can be obtained at www.ICGtesting.com
Printed in the USA
BVOW08s1309120714

358973BV00010B/166/P